"At the moment, there's not much you could con me out of...except my pants."

Skye was pretty sure a smart-ass comment was forming in her subconscious at Nico's words, but then he kissed her, and there were no more thoughts—snarky or otherwise.

There were only his lips—firm and hot, better than she'd imagined. Crazy, whirling sensations formed in her belly. The always-wrong voice in her head was drowned out by the hum of desire that coursed through her.

Nico pulled back and looked at her with half-lidded eyes. "You want me, too, don't you?"

Well, *duh*. But she wasn't going to give him the answer he wanted that easily, even though part of her knew they were at the point of no turning back.

Her dumb instincts were screaming at her to stop, that she barely knew him and casual sex was always a bad idea. So that meant...she had to do the opposite?

Damn straight.

Blaze™

Dear Reader,

I grew up enchanted with the Hollywood version of the California desert—sweeping vistas, endless blue skies and ragtop roadsters. So when I got the chance to write my very own California road story, I was all over it. I live in the California desert now, so my version of the setting is much more real than idealized.

Once Upon a Seduction is also a tribute to fairy-tale romance—complete with a Ferrari as an updated version of the prince's stallion. Fun as it was to write a road story, it was even more fun to write a contemporary fairy tale based on my idea of happily ever after. It's no accident that Skye Ellison is more like me than any other heroine I've written, and I hope you enjoy her journey to happiness as much as I enjoyed writing it.

I love to hear from readers, so drop me a note and let me know what you think of *Once Upon a Seduction.* I can be reached via e-mail at jamie@jamiesobrato.com. Also check out my Web site, www.jamiesobrato.com.

Sincerely,

Jamie Sobrato

Books by Jamie Sobrato

HARLEQUIN BLAZE
  84—PLEASURE FOR PLEASURE
116—WHAT A GIRL WANTS
133—SOME KIND OF SEXY
167—AS HOT AS IT GETS
190—SEXY ALL OVER
216—ANY WAY YOU WANT ME

HARLEQUIN TEMPTATION
911—SOME LIKE IT SIZZLING
997—TOO WILD

ONCE UPON A SEDUCTION

Jamie Sobrato

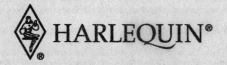

TORONTO • NEW YORK • LONDON
AMSTERDAM • PARIS • SYDNEY • HAMBURG
STOCKHOLM • ATHENS • TOKYO • MILAN • MADRID
PRAGUE • WARSAW • BUDAPEST • AUCKLAND

To my dear friend Bethany Griffin-Faith,
for inspiring me to write my first novel

ISBN 0-373-79241-7

ONCE UPON A SEDUCTION

www.eHarlequin.com

Printed in U.S.A.

1

Once upon a time, in a land not far from L.A., there lived a girl who seemed to have it all.

NO, NO, THAT WASN'T RIGHT. *Have it all* was vague, cliché and boring. And *Once upon a time?* Would an editor even get past that first trite phrase to read the rest of the sentence?

Doubtful.

Skye Ellison glared at the manuscript she'd been struggling with for months. She couldn't get the first line of the story right, so how could she expect to write an entire young adult novel anyone would want to read?

She might as well just face the fact that she sucked the big one and move on to a less creative endeavor, maybe even throw all her efforts into the job she was actually getting paid to do. Now there was a novel idea.

She minimized the document entitled *The Cinderella Solution* and turned her attention to the calendar hanging on her cubicle wall. Today's square was empty, leaving her with two choices—she could start making follow-up harassment sales calls to her on-the-fence customers, or she could wade through the never-ending crapload of interoffice e-mail that flooded her inbox daily. The choices left her with a vague urge to go running out into traffic.

Skye had a theory about cubicles. She believed that if you sat in one long enough, all your thoughts became square. You'd lose your ability to think outside the box, and your creativity would get lost in a haze of geometric shapes and flickering computer screens.

After three tedious years at Dynalux Systems in her six-by-six cubicle, doing work she had trouble explaining to anyone outside the high-tech, pallid-faced world of networking equipment and the people who sold it, this had clearly happened to Skye.

She could no longer even compose a sentence that wasn't an utter and complete cliché. Which was ironic, since she'd taken the mindless job in the first place thinking it would leave her with the mental energy to be creative enough to write novels during her off hours.

In fact, she'd slipped into such a state of crippling boredom at work in the past few months, she'd begun to fear her brain was atrophying. Nothing was going right in her life, she'd made no progress on her book, and she sometimes felt as if she was unable to complete even the simplest of mental tasks.

So when someone dropped a red lace bra on her desk, she couldn't begin to imagine where it had come from. The burst of color alone was shocking enough, but to have something so blatantly sexy right out in the open at her office was an event unheard of since the time Bill Muller tried to spice up the corporate decor by putting a bunch of Hooters Girls posters on his cubicle walls.

"You left this at my house," an unfamiliar male voice said as Skye stared at the bra she'd never seen before.

The only coherent thought she could form was that the cup size looked big enough to accommodate an engorged milk cow.

She looked up from the humongous bra to the source of the voice, and she realized he wasn't so unfamiliar after all. He was someone she knew in passing—Nico Valletti, her ex-boyfriend's landlord. And his expression wasn't exactly congenial. He was one of those guys who smoldered all the time, regardless of whether it was called for or not.

Nico had been blessed with a physical appearance verging on the sublime. A former racecar driver who'd retired early after a famously bad accident on the track, he was gorgeous in the extreme, with nearly black hair, nearly black eyes and a body that could make a girl think dirty thoughts.

And he seemed all too aware of his power over women, as evidenced by his ever-present smirk.

According to Skye's scumbag ex, Martin—or whatever his real name was—Nico had a different girlfriend every week. Sometimes two or three.

She finally found her voice and croaked, "That's not mine. What are you doing with it at my office?"

"Returning it to you, because you've got information I need."

"Are you sure that doesn't belong to one of your girlfriends?"

His gaze traveled from her to the bra and back again. Something about his eyes made her feel as if he had X-ray vision, as if he could see straight through her blouse to her mismatched, no-chance-of-sex-to-day bra and underwear. As if he could tell she didn't own a single red lace bra.

If he made a comment about the fact that the bra on her desk was about four cup sizes away from fitting her, she'd staple him in the hand.

"I'd recognize it if it did," he said in a tone that made her feel like blushing.

If he was telling the truth, then where had the bra come from? Martin had left town three weeks ago, as far as anyone could tell. Not that he'd bothered to say goodbye, or return the money he'd cleared out of her savings account.

She'd been having violent thoughts about her ex ever since that horrifying day when the police had come to her asking questions about him. They'd said Martin was a wanted con artist, that he'd used so many aliases in so many states that no one was sure what his real name was.

She glared up at Nico, wondering if he'd been in on the con. "How did you find out where I work?"

"Your boyfriend mentioned it once, and I'm here to learn what you might know about where he's holed up now."

Her across-the-aisle neighbor and fellow cubicle hater, John Hanson, returned to his desk, watching them. With honey-brown skin and dreadlocks pulled back in a thick ponytail, John was eye-catching, and at six foot four—a couple of inches taller than Nico—he was a little intimidating. He was also Skye's closest friend at Dynalux.

As if he felt the tension in the air, John looked at Nico. "Is there a problem here?"

Skye appreciated his interest, but she wanted to take care of herself. "It's okay, John. We're just talking."

He nodded and sat at his computer, but he kept his gaze locked on Nico for a moment longer—the guy equivalent of a territorial growl.

Skye stood and made like she had work to do elsewhere, grabbing a stack of papers to deliver to destinations unknown. "Whatever I thought I knew about Martin was a lie, so I can't help you."

Nico's eyes narrowed. "You expect me to believe that?"

"How do I know *you* weren't in on his scam? Have the police checked you out yet?"

She tried to walk around him, but he stepped into her path.

"Your boyfriend rips me off, and you accuse me of being part of his con? I'd say *you're* his biggest suspected accomplice."

"Accomplice?" Skye eyed her stapler, wondering how much force it would take to penetrate flesh.

She'd been through hell ever since Martin had run off. And now to have someone suggest she'd been an accomplice in his crime was the cherry on top of her crap sundae.

"I know not to trust appearances, thanks to Martin."

"Well, trust this—he stole ten thousand dollars from my savings account. I'm *not* his accomplice. Now you'll have to excuse me, because I have a job to do."

Being conned by her ex had been the final straw that had convinced Skye all her instincts about men were wrong. If Martin had been the only loser she'd ever hooked up with, then, okay, maybe she could have called it a fluke, but unfortunately, Martin was just one of a long line of losers on Skye's ex list.

She couldn't name a single one of her exes who'd left her with pleasant memories.

She edged around Nico and was a little surprised he let her escape, but then she faced the dilemma of leaving him at her desk alone. What if he stayed?

As if he'd read her mind, he plopped down in her office chair and looked up at her with a grin that didn't quite reach his eyes.

"I can wait," he said.

He certainly could, and then when her boss happened by, he could make her life hell.

She noticed now that she was standing that the scene at her desk had gotten the attention of the entire office. People were peering over cubicles, talking amongst themselves as they cast curious glances at her and Nico. It was only a matter of time before the boss sniffed a lack of productivity in the air and came out to do one of his motivational stalks around the office.

"You have to leave now," she said in a stage whisper.

But instead of doing as she'd asked, he turned around and looked at her computer monitor. That was when Skye remembered the document she'd minimized a few minutes ago—her work in progress. She hurried back into the cubicle and leaned over Nico to grab the mouse, but it was too late.

"What's this?" he asked, covering the mouse with his too-large hand before she could reach it.

"Nothing."

With a click, the first page of *The Cinderella Solution* glowed on the monitor for all the world to read.

"Don't read that!" she said, to no avail.

"Once upon a time—"

"Stop!" Skye felt her face flush. She hated anyone reading her lousy rough drafts and hated getting caught slacking off on the job even more.

"Is this what you do for—" he glanced up at the wall, where the company's logo was emblazoned in royal-blue print "—Dynalux Systems? Write stories?"

"I was taking a break," she lied. "Haven't you ever heard of those?"

"Looks to me like you were slacking. Does your boss know you write stories at work?"

"It's my business what I do on my breaks."

He looked at his wristwatch—an expensive Swiss one, Skye couldn't help noting. "A break at four-thirty in the afternoon? Aren't you about to leave work?"

So she was busted. "I finished all my Dynalux work, okay? Now don't you have a car to go wreck or something?"

He gave her a look. "I wonder how your boss would feel about your slacking, or the fact that he has a probable criminal working for him."

Her manager, Nelson Rudderman, whose favorite words were *maximize* and *strategize,* would have a cow if he found out she was doing something besides *maximizing* her time and *strategizing* how she'd contribute to the future success of Dynalux on company time.

"I'm not a probable criminal," she snapped.

"I don't know that. I think either you tell me where Martin disappeared to, or I'll have to tell your boss about your dirty little secrets."

"I don't have any dirty little secrets, and I have no freaking idea where Martin went."

"You're lying."

Nico might have been hot, but he was a world-class jerk.

"I can call security. You're not even supposed to be in here."

"Go ahead. I'll make sure I talk to your boss on the way out the door."

"What makes you think I'm Martin's accomplice?"

"He talked about you constantly. 'Skye's so hot. Skye's so smart. Skye's gonna write the next big craze in kids' books.' Why would any of that drooling adoration have been an act?"

"Because he wanted you to think he was a nice guy?"

"He could have accomplished that without being so damn annoying. I don't think he would have taken off without a plan to hook up with you again in a few months when the police have forgotten about the two of you."

"Why wouldn't I have just disappeared with him?"

"He's trying to protect you by making it look like you weren't involved."

Skye looked at the bra on her desk. Clearly not hers and apparently not one Nico recognized as a garment he'd removed from any recent dates.

It was just her luck that when she found a guy who was crazy about her, he was also crazy enough to clean out her savings account—not to mention that he was a crazed sex hound who would hump anything in a skirt.

"You're wrong. He was so crazy about me he just couldn't resist taking some other woman's bra off."

"Look, I never said he wasn't a scumbag. But he didn't talk about other women. He talked about you. Constantly. Until I wanted to puke."

Skye blinked away an unwelcome dampness in her eyes. She'd been crazy about Martin, too. Crazy stupid. It was the story of her love life: Skye meets a guy she thinks is great, Skye dates said guy, then said guy takes off with all her money or, at the very least, her dignity.

She'd learned her lesson this time though. Now she knew for absolute sure that all her instincts about men were dead wrong. And she'd vowed that from now on, whenever her instincts told her a guy was right for her, she'd better run in the opposite direction.

For the rest of her post-Martin life, she would live by the rule of opposites. Whatever her instincts told her to do about a guy, she had to do the opposite.

"I don't know what to tell you."

"You're not getting off that easy. Don't you think your employer ought to know what kind of person is working here? Either you cooperate with me, or—"

Skye's temper flared. She hated being backed into a corner, but the truth was, she needed her job, and recent cutbacks at Dynalux surely meant she was being looked at. Sooner or later, the powers that be were going to figure out she wasn't exactly essential to the company. "Or what? You'll get me fired?"

He leveled a gaze at her that was neither friendly nor hostile. "I don't have any control over what your employer decides to do with the information I have."

"What did Martin steal from you?"

"About twenty grand and my favorite motorcycle."

"Isn't that like a drop in the bucket for a racecar driver with a house in Malibu?"

"*Former* racecar driver. And twenty grand is twenty grand."

No point in arguing that. She could, after all, understand his frustration.

He continued. "It wasn't *what* he stole so much as how he stole it. He acted like we were friends, and he lied to me."

"Tell me about it." He'd lied his way into her bed and into her heart. "So what? You're going to hunt him down and demand an apology?"

"I'm going to hunt him down and get my money

back, then turn him over to the cops, since they don't seem all that interested in the case."

"He's probably left the state."

Skye dropped her handful of papers back on her desk, giving up the ruse of having work to do elsewhere.

"You want to know the truth? I think I know where he is. But you do, too, don't you?"

"Right, because I'm his accomplice. I've been looking all my life to hook up with a guy who has five wives in three different states."

Nico shrugged. "I just need some more information to be sure I'm looking for him in the right place."

Dottie Kuzoski got up from her desk three cubicles away and came toward them, her permed ash-blond hair taking on a weird green tinge under the fluorescent light. She slowed her pace as she passed, staring in unabashed lust at Nico. Just when Skye thought she'd leave, she stopped in her tracks and turned around.

"Skye, is this our new rep from the southwest region?"

"No," Skye said and shot Dottie a look.

"Oh. Well. You know, we're not supposed to have personal visitors on company time." She gave Skye a snotty smirk, then smiled at Nico in what must have been her attempt to look seductive. He continued to stare at Skye. "But I won't tell Mr. Rudderman if you don't."

"Thanks, Dottie. I'll be sure to put you in my will."

Skye and Dottie were natural enemies, mainly because Dottie didn't like anyone who got higher sales numbers than her on a regular basis. Not that Skye had ever tried— it was simply a fluke that, without much effort, her mediocre sales numbers consistently topped Dottie's.

Dottie flashed Nico another smile and scurried off, her brown skirt bunching over her ass in an entirely unappealing way.

"Rudderman—that's your boss?"

Skye sighed. "I believe his official title is Big Kahuna."

"I'll give you one last chance to tell me what you know."

He expected her to grovel, to do whatever he demanded? He was messing with the wrong office drone. Dottie had wiped away the last shred of Skye's good humor.

"You can't march in here and accuse me of being an accomplice to a crime and expect me to do whatever you want."

"Maybe I'll just go have a talk with that Rudderman guy then."

He stood and left the cubicle, heading straight for the office Nelly—as she referred to Rudderman when he was out of earshot—occupied near the entrance of the office suite.

"Go right ahead," she blurted to Nico's back, sounding as ridiculous as she felt.

Across the aisle, John was pretending to work, but for a talented wannabe actor, he wasn't doing such a good job of faking it. He had on his headset but hadn't said a word to a customer since he'd returned to his desk. He glanced over at her, and she turned away, ashamed of the misery he might see in her eyes.

Alone in her cubicle, she noticed the red lace bra lying on her desk, mocking her in all its full-figured splendor. She was a 34B on a bloated day, and normally she couldn't have cared less, but at that moment, the bra made her feel somehow inadequate.

She flopped into her chair and saved her manuscript to a disk that was already in the floppy drive, then removed the disk and put it in her bag. She deleted the document from her hard drive, thus eliminating the evidence of her misuse of company time.

So much for her characters finding happily ever after today, or even next month, for that matter. At the rate she was going, she'd end up having to go back to the waitressing work she'd done in college and never again have enough energy to write anything more creative than her yearly holiday see-my-life-doesn't-suck-that-badly newsletter.

Who had come up with the idea of happily ever after, anyway? Probably some giddy lovesick girl back in the Middle Ages when people lived to the ripe old age of thirty-five, and "ever after" wasn't such an ambitious concept. These days, happily *never* after was far more realistic.

2

"Ms. Ellison, I'd like to see you in my office."

Skye recognized that tone. It meant Nelly was drunk on his own power, ready to maximize his opportunity to be a dictator and strategize how he'd make her life miserable. She looked up at him hovering at the entrance of her cubicle and wondered if he practiced making her miserable at home in the mirror in his spare time.

But instead of spouting any of the snarky responses she'd practiced herself in the mirror a time or two, she said, "Um, okay," as her stomach clenched into a cowardly little ball.

She followed him through the maze of cubicles, ignoring the curious stares of everyone they passed. Instead, she focused on Nelly's backside—his saggy posture and the hint of a bald spot on his crown, his wrinkle-free-fabric shirt and the oddly empty seat of his pants.

Had the man been born without butt cheeks? Was that an actual medical condition?

By the time they reached his office, she'd come up with at least five crippling insults to spew at him if he decided to fire her, but she knew she'd never use a single one. Much as she might dislike Nelly, she had a feeling he probably disliked himself even more.

He closed the door and cleared his throat. "Please have a seat."

He walked over to his desk and sat, playing the reigning king of no asses.

"I've been given some unsettling information about you."

"That wasn't my bra," Skye blurted. There were more intelligent things she could have said.

"I'm not talking about a bra, Ms. Ellison." His neck turned hot pink, and Skye wondered if he had a girl-friend, or if having no butt cheeks made romance impossible. "I'm talking about recurrent acts of job delinquency that have been reported to me by a trustworthy source."

"What did that man say to you?" Skye asked, unable to stand the pregnant silence any longer.

"What man? Oh, your visitor on company time? He simply asked where the restroom was—odd, since he could have just asked the receptionist that."

What the hell? Nico hadn't reported her? Or was Nelly lying to her now?

An image of Dottie scurrying around the office appeared in Skye's head, and suddenly she knew for sure who the "trustworthy source" was.

"Have you been monitoring my computer on the LAN again?"

"No, Ms. Ellison. I didn't think I needed to. I thought you understood that company time is reserved strictly for work benefiting Dynalux Systems."

"I do."

"That does not include writing children's stories on my clock."

"I was doing it on break time…sir," she forced herself to add, hoping to gain a few respectful girl brownie points.

Except, if he was lying about having monitored her computer activity, he'd know she'd spent a lot more than her break time writing.

"I'm afraid I have evidence that proves otherwise." Nelly assumed his grave, all-important look.

"Do you know how slow business has been lately?"

Skye's job consisted of, among other pointless and mind-numbing tasks, answering incoming sales calls. People called for information about Dynalux's networking equipment, and Skye's job was to answer their questions and try subtly but swiftly to urge them toward purchasing as much as possible. Sometimes they just asked for brochures or information via e-mail, and sometimes they already knew what they wanted, and she simply had to key in the order.

The job was slightly too complicated for a monkey, but not quite stimulating enough for the average human being to enjoy.

But the powers that be at Dynalux—including Nelly—liked to convolute the process by sending their employees to sales seminars and then urging them to employ the latest covertly pushy techniques to increase revenue.

Skye was so not into it. But it wasn't as if she didn't try. If someone was clearly in need of a router, she'd make sure they got the right one. If, however, they were a clueless grandma from rural Appalachia, who somehow had gotten the mistaken notion that they needed a Dynalux box to connect to their AOL account, she was not going to talk them into buying anything.

She had a conscience, which possibly disqualified

her from ever becoming a wildly successful sales-person.

"I'm fully aware that we're not dealing with a seller's market at this time. But when your incoming calls are slow, there are a number of proactive measures you could be taking."

Right. Follow-up calls. The bane of her slacker sales-girl existence.

"I'm sorry, I'm not doing follow-up calls. If someone needs networking equipment, they'll call us."

Nelly's blood pressure was rising. She could see it in his disturbingly rosy cheeks. "Are you refusing to perform your job?"

"No, I'm just not willing to hassle people in their homes."

"Let me remind you of your job description, Ms. Ellison."

"That's not necessary…sir." Okay, so being respect-ful wasn't one of her strong points.

In her fantasies, this would be where she'd quit. She'd stand up and fling off her headset, which was now dangling around her neck like a high-tech albatross. She'd tell Nelson Rudderman exactly what he could maximize and strategize, and she'd walk out the door. But in her fan-tasies, she'd be earning enough money from writing to pay the rent and wouldn't be suffering this shit job.

And that's why they were called fantasies. She couldn't afford to lose her job right now. She needed to suck it up and appease old Nelly.

"I'm disappointed in your recent performance, Ms. Ellison. You've dropped from being one of our mid-performing sales consultants to hovering in the lowest quarter."

Uh-oh. "I understand. I'll work on improving my sales for the next quarter."

"I don't think you have the best interests of Dynalux at heart."

Did the best interests of Dynalux Systems actually lurk in anyone's heart?

"And I'm afraid the information I was given today is enough for me to terminate your employment here, Ms. Ellison."

"But—"

"Dynalux can't afford to pay employees who aren't interested in doing their best for us."

"I have done my best here," Skye said, her voice veering toward high-pitched and squeaky.

"Then I'm sorry to say your best isn't good enough for Dynalux. You should clear out your desk and vacate the premises immediately."

Skye blinked. She'd just been fired by Nelson Rudderman? In one fell swoop, he'd wiped away all her glorious fantasies of quitting when she finally got her first big book advance. Her instincts—her stupid, faulty instincts—hadn't even seen this coming.

This was the point where she should at least insult him, but she couldn't do it. If Nelly needed to feel important, she didn't have the heart to take that away from him.

"Are we done here?" she said.

He gave her his gravest look and nodded.

Skye kept her expression neutral on her way back to her cubicle. She'd talk to her friends at the office some other time and explain what had happened, but she absolutely would not give Dottie the satisfaction of knowing so soon that she'd been fired.

But Dottie was hovering near her cubicle when she

got there. "What did Mr. Rudderman want?" she asked, her tone verging on gloating.

"He's investigating some instances of theft at the Friday pizza parties. Apparently some cow's been stealing entire pizzas and taking them home for dinner."

Dottie, for once, was speechless. The entire office knew she slipped into the break room every Friday and snuck out with a double sausage pizza all for herself.

"Oh, that's...odd," she finally said, then hurried away.

Across the aisle, John stared at her with his signature look of tired amusement. "You're evil, babe."

"Are my horns showing again?" she joked, surprised at the sudden tightness in her voice.

She absolutely would not start bawling right now.

"What's wrong? Does Nelly have the you're-not-a-go-getter stick up his ass again?"

She nodded, but her stupid lower lip started quivering, and she turned away fast.

"Don't let the bastard get you down," John said, but before he could see how upset she was getting, he got an incoming call. She could tell because he sat up straight and turned on his business voice. "Thank you for calling Dynalux Systems. My name is John. How may I help you?"

She knew that spiel by heart, even heard it over and over again in her dreams after a long day of work. But now she'd have to learn a new mindless spiel, something like, "Would you like to super-size that value meal today, sir?"

Skye grabbed a Nordstom shopping bag from under her desk and began casually gathering her belongings in it. Good thing she didn't keep much at her desk— just a few framed photos of herself with some friends, a Far Side calendar, a bowl of Hershey's Kisses, a battered issue of *Vanity Fair* and a few books that she officially did not read on company time.

Vacating would be easy. She'd been planning her departure since the day she'd arrived.

Figuring out how to pay the rent next month would not be so easy.

Maybe imminent starvation would help her break through her writer's block and finally finish *The Cinderella Solution*. She had to believe that the book had a chance to sell once she got it into the hands of agents and editors. Without a job, she could bump up her usual twenty-pages-per-week goal to something more ambitious. Maybe fifty pages—or seventy-five. That fast a pace would have her finishing the book by the end of the month.

Which still didn't answer the question of how she'd afford her next meal, but Skye would worry about that later. Right now, she had to harness all her frustration and turn it into the thing that would bring her success in her nonexistent writing career. She had to believe she'd sell her first book and many more after that. Then she'd never have to worry about working at a place like Dynalux again.

Her belongings packed up, Skye surveyed the cubicle. All her clients' files would have to be given to other sales consultants, but she'd leave that for Nelly to worry about. And then she spotted the red lace bra lying in the corner. How could she have overlooked it? The thought of touching the thing repulsed her, but she couldn't leave it behind as gossip fodder for Dottie and her cronies, who were not below rummaging through former coworkers' desks.

Skye grabbed a pen and used it to lift the bra. She went

for the garbage can under her desk, but something
stopped her. It was as if, even after his slimy exit from
her life, Martin still had a hold on her. Some other
woman's bra was the only tangible evidence of him left.
At least now she understood his aversion to photo-
graphs—he hadn't wanted to leave proof of his presence
behind.

Sighing, Skye dropped the gigantic bra into her
shopping bag. She'd take it home for a ritual burning,
if nothing else. Or maybe her roommate would decide
to use it in one of her mixed-media art collages.

And now there was nothing left for her to do but slink
out of the office.

Nico Valletti, the jerk… He thought he could strut
into her office and screw up everything? If he hadn't
shown up and ignored that little troll Dottie, she
wouldn't have squealed on Skye, and she'd still have a
job. Nico thought he could mess with her life without
there being consequences?

Okay, so he probably could. What could she do to
him, anyway? She wasn't sure, but she'd think of something. At the very least, she'd let him know exactly
what she thought of his setting off this chain of events.
Why would he appear in her office, say he was going
to get her fired, and then not do it?

It made no sense. But if she happened to accidentally
hurl something at his head in the process of sorting out
the truth, she definitely wouldn't feel guilty.

Not one bit.

Nico drummed his fingers on the steering wheel and
watched the door of the office building. Should he stay
or should he go? That was the question of the minute.

And while logic said to leave and forget the whole problem of Skye Ellison, his guy instincts said to stay. Skye had been haunting his fantasies ever since he'd first laid eyes on her, and something had to give.

He could remember the first time he'd seen her as though it was a classic movie scene.

She'd been walking up the driveway to the cottage on his property last fall, on her way to visit Martin, and she'd been wearing a flippy little dress that was no match for the sea breeze. He'd watched through the window, half amused and half aroused as she'd struggled to keep her pink satin panties covered while her dress flailed in the wind. Damn, but he'd have loved to bring her inside, push that skirt up her thighs, tug off those panties, and bury himself inside her right at that moment.

Her long brown hair had caught his eye for no particular reason except for the way it was tangled around her face in the wind, and he couldn't help admiring her sweet, tight ass as she struggled with her dress. He'd been composing his first witty comment to her when she'd bypassed his door and kept walking toward the cottage.

And that had been the first thing he'd disliked about Martin. Later, listening to him drone on and on about how great Skye was had only made it worse.

But showing up at her office the way Nico just had? Sitting in the parking lot now like a world-class loser? Plotting his next move? He definitely, without a doubt, needed to find a better way to spend his time.

Besides, being inconspicuous while driving a white Ferrari 360 Modena was going to be damn near impossible.

Nico hadn't come to Dynalux planning to follow Skye—if he had, he would have borrowed someone else's car—but after she'd refused to help him and he'd pretended to talk to her boss, he'd left her office unsure what else to do. So here he sat, like a stalker waiting for his next victim.

He had been sure cornering her at her office and threatening to let her boss know about her probable criminal history would be enough to get her to cooperate a little. Catching her slacking off on the job had been icing on the cake, and yet she'd surprised him by not giving in.

Nico suffered a few pangs of remorse over having come here at all, but he figured she'd get a slap on the wrist at worst for having a personal visitor.

Damn it. He couldn't believe he was sitting here, thinking of following a woman whose ass he couldn't stop fantasizing about.

This is what his life had come to. Why hadn't anyone warned him how much retirement would suck?

Oh hell, there he went again letting self-pity creep in. He would not feel sorry for himself. He'd had a great racing career, and he'd chosen when to end it on his own—while he was still at the top. Wrecking his car, breaking his leg in five places and enduring the past year of physical therapy might not have been part of his plan, but he knew he was lucky to have walked away from that wreck alive.

And he had not quit out of fear, as some people had claimed. So what if his father, also a racecar driver, had been killed in a crash twenty years ago? That didn't mean he was afraid of the same fate.

His quitting had simply meant he had enough sense to see a pattern emerging—Valletti men and racing careers resulted in bad news. Driving for Team California in the Indy racing circuit had been his dream come true, but he was ready to move on to the next thing.

Whatever that was.

The entrance of Dynalux Systems opened. Skye came walking out carrying a shopping bag and swiping at her eyes with the back of her hand. As she headed across the parking lot, he could see that she was crying. Bawling, actually, her pretty face contorted in sobs that wracked her shoulders and made him feel like a complete jerk.

Just what he needed. A woman who could turn her emotions on and off like a faucet. Thirty minutes ago, she'd been all smart-ass comments and scathing looks, and now she was crying as if the world had come to an end. Knowing his luck, she'd spotted his car in the parking lot and had emerged from the building already trying to con him again.

He'd never thought of himself as a sucker before three weeks ago. Now, thanks to Martin, or whatever the hell his name was—Nico felt as if he couldn't trust anyone. Especially not the two-faced little hottie who was probably still Martin's girlfriend.

And yet, here he was, torn between wanting to prove she was involved with Martin so he could forget about her, and hoping like hell she wasn't involved so he could get with her himself.

She got into the red Honda del Sol he'd seen parked in his driveway a hundred times, and he knew he was going to follow her. What he'd do when they reached her destination, he had no idea.

Nico waited until she'd pulled into traffic to leave his parking spot, allowing three or four cars between them all the time to make sure she wouldn't notice she was being tailed. The rush-hour congestion on the road gave her little chance to get away from him anyway.

As they sat at what must have been their fifth cycle through the same traffic light, Nico allowed himself to examine his reaction to Skye today. Instead of hating her as much as he'd hoped he would upon confronting her, he'd found himself as mesmerized as ever.

Maybe it was the excitement she stirred in him that was such a draw. Whereas he mostly felt as though he was walking around in a fog, his senses and emotions dulled ever since he'd retired, Skye made him feel completely alive again. How someone he'd mostly viewed from afar could do that, he had no idea. Well, except that a woman as beautiful as her was bound to stir *something* in him.

She had silky brown hair that fell to the middle of her back, long and feminine just the way he liked it. And those eyes, those take-me brown eyes—what man could refuse their unspoken invitation? The clingy top and skirt she wore had given him the chance to admire her very well-shaped curves up close. She clearly spent time at the gym, and he found himself imagining what kind of sweaty workout she did to get such a sexpot body.

He imagined stripping her of her damp little shorts and top, licking the salty perspiration between her breasts, working over her body until her sweat mingled with his, and—

Whoa.

Those were exactly the kind of thoughts he needed to banish. Skye Ellison was likely a con artist herself. Okay, maybe a con artist in training, and possibly not a very good one, but still. She'd probably helped rip him off.

He recalled the way she'd gotten so defensive when

he'd accused her, and that left little doubt in his mind that she at least knew about Martin's scam. The way her hackles had risen at the suggestion of her involvement in the con, she might as well have had a guilty sign blinking over her head. It didn't matter how damn sexy she looked if she was a criminal.

Okay, it was possible he was being paranoid. He couldn't argue that his judgment had been a little off lately, but still, it seemed like a sure bet that Skye was not to be trusted.

Nico scowled at the person who had just pulled up in the emergency lane to the right of him and tried to wedge himself in front of Nico's car. Only in L.A. would anyone be bold enough to try outrunning a Ferrari with a tricked-out Toyota. When the light changed and Nico edged up, coming within inches of hitting the car to keep it out of his lane, he knew he'd finally become an official Los Angelino.

Having moved to the city four years ago to join one of the premier racing teams in the U.S., he'd decided to stick around after he retired from racing. It was easier to film promotional spots from here and he'd gotten attached to his house on the beach.

He missed his hometown sometimes, but he couldn't complain about Southern California's glorious sunshine after having lived through Chicago's miserable winters for most of his life. With only his mother and his sister back in Illinois—neither of whom he was very close to—he hadn't seen any reason to return there.

Right now, in the middle of May, while there was probably a thunderstorm or something happening in the Midwest, it was a sunny, perfect seventy-five degrees in L.A.

After forty-five minutes of following Skye through rush-hour traffic, they finally made it to a North Hollywood apartment complex, where she parked her car. Nico pulled in next to her and got out just as she did.

"What are you doing here?" she said, doing a good job of acting as though she had no idea he'd followed her.

"You didn't think you'd get away that easily, did you?" he said, wishing like hell he'd made a plan.

"I'm thinking I should call the police. Are you stalking me or what?" She began digging around in her bag, then produced a cell phone.

"Go ahead, dial 911. I'm not doing anything wrong."

"Only because being an asshole isn't against the law in the state of California."

"Now that I know where you live, I can really be an asshole if I want to be. Until you agree to help me, that is."

"Fine! You want my help? Go rummage through my underwear drawers. Read my e-mail. See if you can uncover my big fat plot with Martin to steal your money."

"Don't tempt me. How about I just come in and you tell me everything you know."

"I know nothing! When are you going to get that through your head?"

She turned and stalked up the stairs, glancing over her shoulder at him periodically as she went. Her hot little ass tempted and teased him with every step she took.

Then she made her way along the outdoor walkway to her door, number two C, moving as if she were about to break into a sprint.

Nico followed, making a concerted effort to notice his surroundings and not his companion. Skye's white-stucco apartment building was a little shabby, but no more so than the other residences in the area. It was what he'd expect a twenty-something woman to be able to afford in North Hollywood, so no surprises there. The neighborhood was filled with hip young professionals and wannabe actors working their way up to a house in the hills.

Nico had looked at condos in the area when he'd first moved to L.A., but in the end he'd opted for a place away from the city, on the beach in Malibu. The price had been steep, but every time he heard the ocean from inside his house, or glanced outside at the view, he didn't regret his decision. He'd chosen his place partly because of its in-law suite located in a separate cottage, which he could use as a guest house for visiting friends and family.

And the setup had worked out great until Martin had come along and convinced Nico that he was worthy of renting the place while he tried to get his so-called business venture off the ground.

Skye unlocked her door and shot him an incredulous look. "You don't actually think I'm going to let you in?"

Nico shrugged. "I'm an optimist. What do you have to lose by talking to me?"

"Go to hell," she said as she stepped inside the apartment.

Then she slammed the door in his face.

3

AS IF SKYE'S LIFE couldn't get any more bizarre, now she was being stalked by a guy whose car cost more than her entire college education?

Okay, maybe not stalked, but having him pull up beside her in his testosterone-mobile and get out right there in front of her apartment building was a little bit more than her shaky nerves could handle at the moment. She'd driven most of the way home a whimpering, sniveling ball of self-pity, picturing an evening at home with her roommate while they shared their favorite comfort food—a white pizza with extra garlic and mushrooms—and made bad jokes about her employment prospects.

Having an entirely different and unwelcome kind of Italian dish show up on her doorstep had not been part of the plan.

All her instincts were screaming, "Run! Get away from Nico! Don't trust a guy who wears a perpetual smirk!"

But she already knew her instincts, such as they were, sucked the big one. So where did that leave her?

Out of a job, ripped off by her ex, humiliated by a guy who'd gotten famous by driving around in circles really, really fast. Totally unsure what to do with Nico Valletti.

Screwed.

Skye turned around and dropped her bag on the floor, strangely aware of the mystery bra lurking within it. Then she realized she wasn't alone in the living room.

Her roommate, Fiona, was sitting on the couch, her knees drawn up to her chest. "Who was that?"

"Satan."

"I always thought he'd look a little more obvious."

"Apparently he only wears the red devil suit in movies."

Fiona suppressed a smile. "Okay, so is Satan masquerading as any particular human today?"

"Martin's ex-landlord."

"He looked kind of hot—and not in a fire-and-brimstone sense. While you look like hell," she said, staring at Skye's cheeks. "You've got mascara trails."

Skye glanced at herself in the mirror next to the door and saw exactly how ridiculous she looked with her eye makeup streaked down her face. "Just freaking perfect."

"And Satan disguised as Martin's ex-landlord is outside our door because…?"

"Because he thinks I have information that could help him find Martin."

Fiona frowned, then started absentmindedly fiddling with her toe rings. That's what she always did when she was deep in thought.

"Whatever you're thinking, stop it." Skye had learned the hard way that Fiona's advice on life matters great and small often led to unexpected results. Skye's recent highlighting debacle at the hair salon was a case in point.

"You don't even know what I was thinking about."

"It doesn't matter. I don't want to hear about it."

"You're still mad at me about those highlights, aren't you?"

Skye ignored the question, took off her shoes and headed for the kitchen, praying there was still a Diet Coke left in the fridge.

"I still think platinum is a good color on you," Fiona called after her.

One lonely bottle of Diet Coke stood in the refrigerator door, as if the beverage gods knew she'd need some caffeinated comfort. She grabbed it and returned to the living room, where Fiona had moved on from her toe rings to wrapping one of the two braids she had her hair in today around her fingers. Hair fiddling represented Fiona's deepest level of thought and was normally reserved for creative endeavors, such as when she had an idea for a new collage.

"I hope you're deep in thought about art and not my life."

Skye sank into her favorite purple chair and propped her feet on the matching ottoman. For the first time, she noticed that Fiona was listening to some strange jungle-sounds CD and watching CNN at the same time. An assortment of odd objects—everything from boa feathers to bottle caps—lay scattered on the coffee table in front of her. This meant she was trying to get new ideas for her work.

"Sorry, I'm interrupting your brainstorming with my life drama, aren't I?" That was the thing about living with an artist—it was hard to tell if she was working or just sitting on the couch.

Fiona shrugged and stopped playing with the braid. She had long black hair, pale skin and luminous green eyes, but what turned heads everywhere she went was her confidence. She was so self-possessed, so comfortable in her skin, she could wear her hair in pigtails and make it look sexy. Skye envied that.

"What would I have for entertainment if not your guy problems?" Fiona said.

"I am so screwed."

"Because of Satan? Why don't you just talk to him and tell him everything you know about Martin. Then he'll leave you alone."

"That's not why I'm screwed. I just got fired."

Her eyes widened. "Fired from Dynasucks? What happened?"

"I don't want to talk about the lurid details right now." Skye took a long drink of her Diet Coke, blatantly breaking her recent pact with Fiona to drink only natural, unprocessed fluids.

"Does it have something to do with that Satan guy?"

"Yes—well, no. I don't know," Skye said. Not that she'd helped matters by giving her boss every reason in the world to fire her.

"Did you tell Nelly to go screw himself?"

"No, I totally wimped out."

"Why?" Fiona had been subject to enough of Skye's rants about what she'd say to Nelly on the day she left Dynalux to deserve an answer, but Skye wasn't sure she had a decent one.

She shrugged. "Because I want to be polite to the people who attempt to ruin my life?"

Fiona shook her head but said nothing.

"Stop with the disapproving silence!"

"You'll find a better job. I saw a help wanted sign at Starbucks this morning," she said. It was Fiona's lame version of a joke.

"You went to Starbucks? What happened to your disavowing all unnatural beverages?"

Fiona managed to look chagrined—not one of her more common emotions. "Coffee beans are natural. Sort of."

"I can't take another sales job. I think I'd rather turn tricks."

"You're way too much of a wuss to be a hooker."

"Do you have any better ideas?"

"There's always waitressing. I could talk to Tommy at Club Sunset and beg him to give you a job again."

Skye sighed. She'd be back where she'd started in college. She and Fiona had met five years ago when they were both waitresses at the bar and grill where Fiona still worked. But what other option did she have?

None at the moment.

"I'll be forever in your debt, Fi."

"I'm working tonight. I'll talk to him then," she said, but the ironic look she gave Skye told the truth about the situation.

It sucked.

Skye had left the job and Club Sunset three years ago with a vow never to go back, she'd been so sure she was moving on to bigger things. The thought that all this time had passed and she still hadn't sold a book…

It was too depressing to dwell on. Maybe she'd never sell a book. Maybe being a sales consultant for Dynalux Systems was the best job she'd ever have, and she'd just thrown it away because she was too proud to grovel.

"I'll talk to Tommy on one condition—you spill the story of how you got fired."

A few more gulps of Diet Coke, and the soothing effects of caffeine began to calm Skye's nerves. She told

Fiona about everything except the bra—which she was reserving for dramatic effect.

"Okay," Fiona said when she finished. "You're leaving something out."

"What do you mean?"

"I got a glimpse of Satan," Fiona said, her tone pregnant with meaning.

"And?"

She narrowed her eyes at Skye. "And you know he's a hottie."

"What does that have to do with anything?"

"We both know how you get around gorgeous men."

"So?" she asked, but she knew what Fiona meant.

Skye's faulty instincts were at their worst when a beautiful man was involved. Martin had been the kind of guy women stopped and turned around to admire when he passed them on the street, and he'd also been her biggest guy disaster.

"What are your instincts telling you to do about him?"

"Run, run, run, as fast as I can."

Fiona's brow furrowed. She'd helped Skye develop her new do-the-opposite strategy. "That's weird. Then... you have to give him a chance."

"A chance to what? Ruin what's left of my sad little train-wreck life?"

"I mean you have to cooperate with him, if your instincts are telling you not to. Besides, you said yourself Martin is nowhere near the top of the police's priority list. If someone doesn't find him soon, he'll probably never be found."

"That's what I'm afraid of."

"In fact—a guy as hot as Satan, and your instincts are telling you to run? You may need to take him straight to bed and screw his brains out if you really want to stick with the rule of opposites."

"Fiona! That's insane."

"Think about it. You're always taking things slow, getting to know the guy before you do the deed, waiting for love, blah, blah, blah. Maybe that's all your crappy instincts leading you astray."

"Or maybe it's just, like, common sense. Like, what ninety percent of the human race calls the courtship process!"

"I'm just saying, with your track record… This is your first chance to test out your theory. You ought to do it right."

"Right," Skye said, panic settling in her belly.

She didn't want to test out any theories, especially not with a guy who'd practically gotten her fired from her crappy job. Although…

It was possible she needed to face the fact that her own actions, more than anything else, were what had caused her to lose her job. Nico's appearance had simply hurried the process along.

"Go talk to him. Maybe between the two of you, you really can find Martin and get your money back."

"Or maybe he'll turn out to be a psychopath, and weeks from now the police will find pieces of me scattered around the foothills—the pieces the mountain lions didn't eat, anyway."

"If he were a true psychopath, he wouldn't have approached you in broad daylight, at your office, with a zillion witnesses to ID him and describe your heated exchange to the police."

"You haven't seen what he brought and left on my desk." Skye retrieved her bag and pulled out the red bra, then held it up in all its glory. "Would any sane man think this belongs to me?"

Fiona gawked at the size of the thing. "Why would he bring you that?"

"He thought it was mine, left behind in Martin's cottage. It was his excuse to pay me an office call."

She frowned. "I thought Martin didn't leave any traces when he left."

"Actually, he did leave a weird assortment of junk at his place, but nothing that could really lead us to him."

"Why'd you bring that home?"

Skye frowned at the bra. "I thought we might want to perform a ritual burning. You know, to rid my life of the last physical trace of Martin."

"Sorry, but ever since the drunken flaming-dildo incident, I've sworn off ritual burnings."

Skye laughed in spite of her bad mood. Fiona had nearly burned down their apartment getting rid of the evidence of a previous boyfriend, who'd surprised her with an oh-so-romantic gift-wrapped dildo for Valentine's Day—that he'd wanted her to use on him.

"Let me see that," Fiona said, reaching for the bra. "Maybe it'll fit me."

"Right." Skye tossed the bra to her. "In your pornstar dreams."

Fiona held the triple-D-cup bra up to her C-cup chest. "It's close."

"Right. If you talk into it, there'll be an echo."

She turned the bra around and read the tag. "Lolita's Creations, Las Vegas, Nevada. Size 34DDD. Wow, I'd be surprised if the owner of this can stand upright without assistance."

"That's kind of odd—a city name on a bra tag?"

"Maybe it's a custom lingerie shop. I mean, look at this thing. It's got some unusual details."

There was a tiny beaded butterfly between the cups, and the edges were trimmed in sequins.

"I wonder…" Skye said, not quite ready to get her hopes up.

"If this is a clue to Martin's whereabouts? It could be." Fiona looked at the tag again. "The only other information is Dry Clean Only."

"Why would anyone wear a dry-clean-only bra?" Skye asked as Fiona handed the bra back to her.

"Maybe if it's, like, their professional attire?"

"So my ex was screwing a stripper, a show girl or a prostitute. That makes me feel so much better."

"Don't forget porn star."

"Thanks for reminding me."

"Why don't you at least find out if Satan's idea about Martin's whereabouts matches up with your little lingerie clue?"

Her clue was hardly little, but Fiona did have a point.

"Okay, fine. I'll talk to him, but if it's a disaster, I'm giving you fifty percent of the blame."

"Does Satan have a human name?"

"Nico Valletti, if you can believe it. He should be a soap opera star instead of a stalker."

"Maybe Nico's still lurking outside waiting for you."

Skye tried to ignore the butterflies whirring in her belly as she stood, dropped the bra in her purse and put her shoes back on. "He drives a Ferrari," she said, not sure what that suggested about his disaster potential.

"And he lives in Malibu. You could do worse."

"Fiona, I'm going to talk to him about Martin, not scope him out as a possible rebound guy."

"Every guy that rich and gorgeous has the potential for something."

"I thought you had more integrity than me."

Fiona grabbed the remote and switched off CNN, leaving just the jungle sounds to punctuate their conversation. From the distant tropics, a monkey screeched.

"I'm turning thirty next month," she said. "The starving artist thing is getting old, and I don't think it would be so bad to be with a guy who doesn't have to go Dutch on every date."

Skye blinked. She'd never thought she'd hear Fiona sounding so…pragmatic.

"What happened to, 'Thirty is the year when we finally become real women'?"

"It is, and as a real woman, I think I'd like to have some financial stability in my life."

"What are you saying?" Skye's head was starting to do the same bongo-drum thing it did when she drank too many margaritas. Or maybe that was part of the jungle-sounds CD.

"This probably isn't a good time to spring this on you," Fiona said as she began to rearrange the found objects on the coffee table. "But I've decided to leave Club Sunset and take that pharmaceutical sales job my dad found for me."

Skye sat on the ottoman, her beleaguered brain ready to call it quits for the day. She'd thought she'd always have Fiona to be her fellow starving artist. And all through the years, even though she was five years older than Skye, Fiona was the one who'd never seemed to mind being a waitress and earning petty cash here and there on her collages. She'd seemed to relish her carefree lifestyle.

"You? In sales?"

She shrugged. "Just until I set the art world on fire."

"But—"

"Please don't look so disappointed. I've given this a lot of thought."

Skye produced a shaky smile. "Sorry, I'm just a little shocked. But you're right, you'd be a fool to pass up the money."

"At least we know there'll be an opening at Club Sunset," Fiona said, and that was the final straw.

"Excuse me," Skye said.

She stood up and hurried into the bathroom to wash her face, returned and grabbed her bag, then hurried toward the door before she could burst into tears again.

"Skye? Are you okay?"

"I'm fine, I just need some fresh air," she said, flashing a shaky smile at Fiona before she disappeared.

Outside, Nico was nowhere to be seen, and it was all for the best. She couldn't have faced him now anyway without revealing herself as the basket case she actually was.

Skye drove on autopilot, her thoughts bouncing from one disastrous event to the next, tears prickling her eyes again as she navigated the road without thinking about it.

God, she'd turned into a caricature of a twenty-something. Job problems, guy problems, roommate problems…

She wasn't sure where she was going, but she knew she didn't want to go anywhere she'd already been. A half hour later, she was miles down the freeway, taking the Malibu exit to Martin's house.

Well, actually, to Nico's house. Who knew if he was home, but it was her turn to stalk him, regardless.

NICO DIDN'T KNOW whether to be relieved or frustrated that now he had no excuse not to put Skye out of his thoughts. But of course, if it was as easy as all that, he'd have forgotten about her weeks ago.

He closed his front door, kicked off his shoes, and walked through the house to the living room, which mocked him with its emptiness. Why the hell had he come home, anyway?

Because the thought of going out to dinner alone, or picking up carry-out alone, or sitting in a bar alone, might have meant crossing the thin line between sane and crazy. He'd always relished his single status, until the accident. Since his recovery, he'd continued to date, but the women who'd once amused him simply by being hot and willing were now not so satisfying.

Getting a glimpse of his own mortality could do that to a guy.

That hadn't stopped him from seeking the company of women, but lately, all the company had been strictly sexual. And none of them seemed to care one way or the other.

The light on his answering machine was flashing, and the LCD said he had three messages, so he hit the play button and listened.

"Hey, Nico, busy tonight?" a woman's voice said. He didn't recognize her right away. "It's Lisa. Call me if you'd like some company."

Lisa. Lisa who? He felt a little pang of disgust at himself for not knowing. *Company* was the word he did know though—it was the universal booty-call code word.

A second message began to play. "Nico, hi. It's me, Dawn. Just wondering if you'd like some company tonight."

There it was again. That word.

A third message. "Hi, Nico. It's Misha—"

He stopped the recording before he had to hear it again.

And for the first time, he realized what was bothering him so much. He'd become one of those guys. A guy women didn't want anything serious with—a guy they didn't even want to talk to or go out to dinner with. A guy they just wanted to screw.

How the hell had that happened?

Sure, he'd expected retirement from racing to bring with it a fading of the limelight, but he hadn't expected women to stop regarding him as an interesting human being outside of the bedroom.

He sank onto the couch, propped his feet on the coffee table, and grabbed the remote. With the press of a button, a sixty-inch plasma TV screen emerged from a console cabinet on the other side of the room, and with another press of a button, the sports channel was on, displaying scores from yesterday's games.

He needed to order a pizza, do something for dinner, but the thought of eating alone… Best not to think about it again. Instead, he watched the sports news and tried really hard to give a damn about any of it. Tried to ignore his annoyance that he wasn't making news anymore.

Thoughts of Skye invaded—a welcome distraction from the news. He closed his eyes and summoned an image of her at her desk at work. He'd never been big on office fantasies, but he could have thought of a few ways to liven up that cubicle of hers. He could have

shown up after hours…found her working alone…
propped her up on that desk…pressed himself between
her legs. He imagined the silky feel of her, the way her
thighs would clench around his hips, the way the flesh
of her breasts would mold to his hands, the way her
breath would feel tickling his neck as he pounded
against her—

Then the doorbell rang and jarred him back to reality.
He got up from the couch, adjusted his pants, and went
to the door slowly, as if he didn't care about having a
visitor, not sure whether to be happy or disgusted that it
was probably some unannounced booty call dropping by.

And when he saw Skye outside the foyer window
standing on his front steps, it was the most welcome
sight he'd beheld in a long time. An unexpected burst
of joy surged in his chest. Again, Skye evoked in him
emotions that he'd been afraid might be gone for good.

She was glaring at the door, not exactly looking
happy to be there. Which was too bad. If she'd been on
his doorstep looking for sex and nothing more, she was
the one woman he'd be more than happy to oblige.

But more likely, his lure had worked. She wanted to
know if he really knew where Martin was. He didn't
know, but he had a damn good idea.

He opened the door and smiled.

"You bastard, your showing up at my office set off
the chain of events that got me fired, and you expect me
to help you?"

"You got yourself fired. And hello to you, too."

"I didn't come here to chitchat. Are you going to let
me in, or should I just stand out here until I blow away?"

Nico stepped aside, images of the first time he'd seen
her struggling with her skirt filling his head, her tempting

proximity causing his groin to stir again. "Downside of living on the ocean. The wind can be a bitch."

She turned on him and shot him a screw-you glare. "How about you say something more like, 'I'm sorry you've lost your only source of income. I'll be thinking of you when you're living on the street.'"

"By the looks of that place, I'd say I did you a favor. Sit in a cubicle like that long enough and you'll go insane."

Her expression transformed for a few seconds, as if she was shocked by his observation. But then she recovered.

"I don't need your career advice."

"You didn't come here to scold me about your lost job, did you? Because I have a feeling that Dottie chick is the one you need to scold."

"No, I came to beg your forgiveness for breathing." She leveled a smart-ass gaze at him that made him want to kiss her senseless.

He had to start thinking with the right head. Fast. She was too damn sexy when she was pissed.

"Could it be you want to see if I really know where Martin is?"

She shrugged. "If you know where he is, then why haven't the police beaten down his door?"

She was smarter than he'd hoped.

"I've told them everything I know, but I'd say Martin has left the state and is no longer high on their priority list."

"What you mean is, you don't have a clue where to find him."

"The way I see it, you're in a win-win situation. Either you help me out because you want to find Martin as much as I do, or you help me out because you need to keep me away from your scumbag boyfriend."

"So what if I agree to help you? Then what?"

Nico had asked himself that question many times already. He might have been able to take whatever information he could get from Skye and find Martin on his own, but he wouldn't have much chance of getting close to him once he found him. Skye, on the other hand, was quite possibly Martin's Achilles' heel.

And even if she wasn't, she was the best bait he could hope to find to lure Martin out of hiding.

"Then we go on a little trip."

"Go where?"

"I can't reveal all my secrets up front."

"You expect me to just take off with you? Some guy I don't even know?"

"Don't I look trustworthy?"

"No."

"Can you even trust your own judgment after dating a con artist?"

One corner of her mouth curved up, and Nico knew he almost had her.

"I might be willing to help except I'm broke, and I need to be looking for a job right now since I'm newly unemployed."

Okay, so he wasn't a heartless ogre. Another stab of guilt struck him that she'd lost her job, and in spite of his suspicions about her, he felt as though he ought to help somehow. "So you're a writer. Can't you get a job doing that?"

"Yeah, me and the five zillion other people who want to be writers. I can just go down to the book factory and fill out an application. They're always hiring."

"You live in L.A. Why aren't you writing for Hollywood like everyone else?"

She pinned him with a look. "For one, not everybody wants to write for Hollywood, and second, it's not that simple."

"Okay, okay. I know writing jobs don't grow on palm trees, but still, if you've got any talent, you should be able to get work."

"Screw you."

Nico held up his hands in surrender. "Guess I had that coming. Listen, if it turns out you aren't involved with Martin, I'll get you some face time with my next-door neighbor. He's the CEO of a couple of TV networks. He's always complaining about how there's no talent in Hollywood."

He could see the spark of interest in her eyes that she was probably trying really hard not to show.

"Okay, whatever. That's not going to pay my bills right now."

"I'll cover your expenses until you can pay me back."

Her expression transformed to suspicious, but she made no further protest.

"So it's a deal," he said before she could change her mind. "You might want to pack for hot weather. We'll have to take a little drive."

"How little?"

"We could get there in six hours or less."

She seemed to be doing the math in her head. Six hours or less could mean driving to any number of places—San Francisco, Las Vegas, San Diego, Mexico, Arizona or anyplace in between.

"You have to at least tell me where we're going."

"Does it matter?"

"I might have a clue about where Martin is."

Nico stared at her, daring her to look away. She

didn't seem much like a criminal, but then neither had Martin. He'd seemed like a regular guy, a friend even. And Nico was the dumb-ass who'd fallen for Martin's story of needing a loan to get his business venture up and running and having an ex who'd ruined his bank credit.

"What's your clue?"

"Did you bother to inspect this bra?"

Nico shrugged. "My expertise is in bra removal, not inspection."

She tried not to laugh but failed. "So is that why you thought it might fit me?"

"For all I know, you like to stuff your bra with basket-balls."

Though he'd seen her coming and going from the cottage enough to know she didn't bother with anything more figure-enhancing than a push-up bra, and she was sexy as sin regardless. The red bra had just been his excuse for coming to see her, and of course, he'd wanted to make sure she knew Martin had been anything but worthy of her affection, not only because of his thievery but also because he screwed around.

She dug around in her bag and pulled out the bra, then held it out to him.

"The tag says it was made in Las Vegas. Is that where you think Martin is?"

Nico kept his expression neutral. He wasn't sure how much he really wanted Skye to know. If she was still hooked up with Martin, she'd be able to warn him that they were coming. But the truth was, he had a good hunch Martin was in Vegas. It was like the Olympic Games for con artists, their ultimate challenge, and the police had agreed that even if Vegas wasn't his goal, he likely could have made a stop there on the way to his next destination.

"Actually, no," Nico lied. "There's this town up in the high desert that I saw on Martin's phone bill before the police took away the evidence."

That part, at least, was true. Elroy, a nowhere town in the middle of the Mojave, had shown up twice on the bill. And since it was on the way to Vegas, Nico figured it warranted a stop-off.

"What town?"

"Like I said, can't reveal all my secrets at once."

She pursed her lips, then sighed. "If I go, I want my own private room wherever we stay, and you pay all trip expenses."

"Of course." He didn't see any reason to point out that if he had his way, they'd only need one bed.

If he was destined to be the kind of guy women wanted for one thing only, he might as well have his fun with the one woman he wanted most.

"And no more suggesting I'm in cahoots with Martin, because I'm not."

Nico shrugged. He didn't believe her for a second. "Whatever you say, babe."

"I'm serious."

"So am I."

"So what? We just get in the car and take off?"

"We should probably pack first," he said, hardly believing she'd agreed to go. "I'll pick you up first thing tomorrow morning."

"This is insane."

That was one thing they could agree on.

Wanting a woman he shouldn't, depending on her to help him find a guy he had only the shakiest clues to the whereabouts of, hoping she'd either prove herself repulsive or completely uninvolved with Martin within the space of the next few days—that was his dilemma and his reward, all rolled up in one hot, tempting, pain-in-the-ass package.

4

"HAVE YOU BEEN sniffing my collage adhesive?"

Skye hadn't expected her roommate to be thrilled that she was hopping in a car and leaving town with Nico tomorrow morning. But what she needed right now was moral support—not accusations of illegal use of art supplies.

She ignored Fiona and headed straight for her bedroom before she could be talked out of the craziest thing she'd agreed to do in this lifetime. Already, the idea of doing the opposite of what her instincts told her was feeling ridiculous, foolhardy—impossible.

But she had to give it a try. What other options did she have? What had her old way of making decisions gotten her but heartache and failure?

She and Fiona had developed the theory after Skye had found out about Martin's deception, and in the tequila-laced fog of those depressing days, it had seemed perfectly sound. Maybe there were a few holes in their logic, she had to admit now, but she'd never know if the theory of opposites worked until she applied it to her life.

And without a job or a dime in her savings account, was it really so crazy to go looking for Martin? What else did she have to lose?

Not much. And she couldn't deny the lure of Nico's promise to hook her up with that TV guy. Scriptwriting might not have been her focus, but it would be a huge step in the right direction. Such impressive writing credits would surely open doors that could lead to her selling *The Cinderella Solution.* Hope surged in her chest at the very thought.

She flipped on the overhead light in her bedroom, then tugged open her top dresser drawer. Instinct told her to pack all the travel basics—versatile cotton pieces, comfortable underwear, walking shoes—so that meant she had to do the opposite.

She grabbed all her laciest, most impractical undergarments and tossed them on the bed, then headed for her closet, flung it open, and pulled out the most Vegas-appropriate clothes she owned. A pink pair of capri pants with beaded fringe around the leg openings, a stretchy black mini skirt, a red glittery tank, a white halter top, a black going-out-clubbing dress that she hadn't gotten a chance to wear yet, plus a few more pieces. She turned with the pile of clothes draped over her arm to find Fiona gaping at her.

"Are you going to find Martin or are you running away to become a showgirl?"

"Okay, so tell me how far I have to take this 'doing the opposite' thing? Does it apply to underwear choices and packing for trips, too?"

"Of course not!" She frowned. "Well, but, maybe you're onto something there."

"Maybe the further I take the philosophy, the more completely my life will be transformed."

"This is wacked," Fiona said, shaking her head. "I mean, if you take this too far, you'll end up sitting in restaurants ordering liver and onions when you want to eat a cheeseburger."

She had a point there. Skye had to draw the line someplace, but where? Maybe whenever her decisions could directly impact her relationships with men. So, in that case, clothes, hair and makeup were an issue—cheeseburgers were not.

Skye dragged her leopard-print overnight bag out of the bottom of her closet and opened it on the bed. There was enough room for a weekend or more worth of clothing in the bag, but would she need more than that? She hadn't even bothered to ask Nico how long they'd be gone. Maybe he didn't know either.

"Okay, so the rule of opposites only applies to decisions that affect my love life. How's that?"

"Sounds…reasonable," Fiona said. "But I think we need a litmus test to determine if the theory really works or not."

"You mean like, if my Prince Charming shows up out of nowhere with a glass slipper that magically fits my foot—"

"No, but if you're really making decisions that are the opposite of your relationship instincts, and all of a sudden you find yourself with a great guy who gives you multiple orgasms and is head over heels in love with you, you'll know it's working."

"But at any moment, the relationship could turn into a disaster. Doesn't there need to be, like, a time limit or something? Maybe things have to be going well for a year, or two years…"

Fiona made a sour face. "I don't want to wait that long to find out if we're right. I'd say a month of dating bliss is plenty to prove the theory."

"Okay, a month of multiple orgasms with Mr. Perfect, and a confession from him of undying love."

She waited for Fiona's enthusiastic agreement, but instead received silence.

And then, "Listen, Skye. I don't know about you taking off for destinations unknown with a guy you barely know. I mean, it's possible we're wrong on this doing-the-opposite thing. Maybe you've had the world's longest string of bad luck, and maybe it's due to end any second now. Maybe you don't need to do a thing."

"The last thing I need is you getting wishy-washy on me now. You came up with the whole damn idea in the first place!"

Skye grabbed her bras and panties from the bed and flung them into the bag to punctuate her statement. She would not be deterred.

"Okay, you're right. You're just freaking me out here. I never imagined you'd embrace the plan so thoroughly, you know?"

"I just feel like I've screwed up most of my life up until now. My love life's in the toilet, and now my work life is, too. And I'm running out of excuses. If things don't start looking up soon, I'm going to have to face the fact that I'm a loser."

She flopped down on the bed and looked at her assortment of hoochie-mama attire with disgust. Fiona sat beside her and draped an arm over her shoulders. She leaned her head against Skye's and sighed.

"You're anything but a loser, babe. Of all the people I know, you're one of the few who's had the courage to really go after your dreams. You took a lousy job that wasn't at all suited to you, just so you'd have the energy to write at night. And so what if you're not where you want to be yet? You're only twenty-five—you've got your whole life ahead of you."

"My whole life minus twenty-five years," Skye said, then felt like a jerk for being so melodramatic when Fiona herself was about to take the kind of job she'd sworn she'd never be caught dead in.

"Yeah, well, as a woman almost five years your senior, I can tell you, you've got a long way to go before you can ever think about giving up."

"So is age thirty the cut-off date for wholeheartedly pursuing my dreams?"

"Not funny."

"I'm sorry. I'm being a bitch. Feel free to smack me."

"How about I help you add a few things to your wardrobe selection there to ensure you won't have people mistaking you for a hooker?"

"And then can we go out for a white pizza at Luigi's?"

"Absolutely. I'll call Sammy and Leila and see if they want to join us, okay?"

Skye felt herself relaxing a bit for the first time all evening. A dinner at her favorite pizza place with her three favorite people was just what she needed right now. And with any luck at all, she'd be able to forget about Nico Valletti for the rest of the night.

THE FERRARI'S ENGINE rumbled to a stop in front of Skye's apartment building, and Nico peered out the window at the landing in front of her door. What the hell was he doing? Did he really think taking off on a road trip in search of a con man with said thief's probable con-artist girlfriend was going to get him anything but royally screwed?

That was the thing about retirement. He had too much time on his hands. He needed to start doing some volunteer work, become a mentor to troubled teens or something like that. He'd had good intentions, but somehow, he'd managed to let time slip by him recently, unaware of its passing until he'd forgotten an appointment or missed calling his mother on her birthday.

Nico got out of the car and stretched, his body still stiff from a restless night's sleep. He'd been unable to get Skye and the trip off his mind, and now, in the muggy, still morning air, he wished like hell he'd taken a sleeping pill.

He headed up the stairs to Skye's apartment. When he knocked on the door and a woman he didn't recognize answered, he glanced at the number beside the door frame to be sure he was in the right place.

"You must be Satan," she said.

Um, okay.

She was tall and lanky, sexy in that raw way that certain women had. They tended to be the ones who could sit around all day naked just as comfortably as they could wearing clothes. She wore her dark hair in two long braids, and her tank top and faded jeans hugged nice curves.

"No, actually, I'm Nico. Is Skye here?"

"Sorry, I'm Fiona, Skye's roommate. I was joking about the Satan thing. She's in her bedroom second-guessing her wardrobe choices for the trip."

Nico studied her expression to see if it matched her sarcastic tone, but he couldn't tell. He moved past her into the apartment and found himself in the middle of a room with lavender walls, dark purple furniture, and red pillows strewn every which way. Some crazy-looking paintings with stuff glued to them hung in various spots around the room, and the overall effect was girly overload. Nico had the strange sensation that he was going to emerge from the apartment smelling like a woman—as had happened to him in the past when he'd accidentally tossed a shirt into a bowl of a girl-friend's potpourri during a moment of passion.

"Come on back," Fiona said, leading him toward a hallway, and then to Skye's bedroom.

"Your ride's here," she said to Skye, her voice laced with sarcasm again. She stood staring from him to Skye and back again, clearly not shy about eavesdropping.

Skye turned to face him, looking as amazing as ever. She wore her hair pulled back in a thick ponytail that hung down the middle of her back, and she had on a pair of white capri pants and a little pink tank top that would make it hard for him to keep his gaze from wandering south.

"Hi," she said, then turned back to her travel bag, giving Nico the pleasure of letting his gaze roam wherever it wanted for now. "I'll be ready in just a sec."

"No hurry. I just heard on the radio there's an accident in the Cajon Pass. Sounds like we might be stuck on this side of the mountains for a while."

Not hitting any major traffic in L.A. was about as likely as the smog vanishing from the sky. It just didn't happen. The Cajon Pass was the passage from the L.A. basin up the mountains into the high desert, where seedy towns offered little more than fast food and bad motels for travelers on their way to Vegas. Searching those towns for Martin sounded anything but appealing, but if they had to do it, he could think of worse people to do it with than Skye.

"Maybe we shouldn't leave until later then," Skye said, staring forlornly at a laptop computer that sat in a carrying case on her bed.

"I think we ought to just take our chances. The accident could be cleared up by the time we make it to the pass."

Skye was looking at him now as if she didn't really see him.

"Is something wrong?" he asked.

"Oh, nothing. I mean, yeah, there is. I'm just kind of freaked out about this whole trip. And I should be staying home writing, not chasing after my ex."

"So bring your computer with you and write during downtime."

Nico knew there was a danger of her second-guessing the whole trip and deciding not to go. He'd worried that she might change her mind, but really, what did she have to lose by going? If she was in cahoots with Martin, she could go along presumably to keep tabs on Nico. While on the other hand, if Martin had scammed her, too, and she didn't try to find him, she could definitely kiss her life savings goodbye.

"Okay, I'll bring the computer. It might come in handy if we end up in any hotels that have Internet access."

"I don't have much trunk space, but it should fit behind one of the seats if nothing else," Nico said as he grabbed her two bags from the bed and hefted them onto his shoulders.

He realized belatedly that her bringing her computer along would offer him access to her private life—and, he hoped, evidence of her true relationship with Martin. He just needed to get some time alone with the laptop, and he could check out her e-mail, her Internet use, her saved documents. Maybe something would tell him what he needed to know—to trust Skye, or not to trust her.

They walked to the front door, and from the couch Fiona called, "You two kids be careful now, you hear?"

"Bye," Skye called back.

"Call me!"

Nico waved as they walked out the door, and a minute later, they were standing behind the Modena trying to fit Skye's bags in with his.

"We could take my car, you know."

"No way." Cars like this one were made to be driven through the desert on empty stretches of highway. It had been too long since he'd gotten it out on a good road trip, and he wouldn't miss this chance.

After some shuffling, everything fitted. He opened the passenger door, and Skye climbed in and stared up at him as if she'd just boarded an alien space craft.

"Are you sure you want to travel through the desert in this thing? Aren't you afraid of it getting stolen or something?"

He ignored her and closed the door, then went to the driver's side and got in.

"It's got a security system," he finally said, turning the key in the ignition. "Besides, thieves usually steal common cars, not exotics."

With that statement, the engine revved to life, a deep, throaty rumble that sounded like no other car on the road.

"You must be kind of a show-off, to want to ride around in this thing."

He cast a put-out look at her. "I like fast cars, in case you couldn't guess from my last profession."

Skye put on her seatbelt and adjusted her seat, as they headed toward the freeway.

"I heard about your accident, but I don't really know any of the details," she said. "What happened?"

Nico winced. He hated telling the story, hated admitting that he didn't really remember much from the most pivotal moment of his life.

"My left front wheel clipped the wall, is my best guess. The contact caused me to lose control, and the next thing I remember is waking up in the hospital with a mangled leg and a bunch of aching body parts."

The part of the story he never told was that he'd woken up so thankful to be alive, so thankful he hadn't suffered his father's fate, he couldn't summon the desire to ever get back on a race track. It wasn't fear—he still loved to drive, and he still loved fast cars—but he had this sense that he'd been given a second chance at life, and for reasons he couldn't put into words, racing wasn't part of the second chance. He was too grateful to still be alive to test fate again.

"Why did you stop racing?"

Nico didn't answer for a while, and then, without really planning to, he found himself telling her. Saying the words he never said out loud.

"I don't know why, but I just came out of the whole thing feeling like I wasn't supposed to get back on the track again. Like I'd been given my big hint to move on to the next phase of my life."

"Which is what?"

"Hell if I know."

He could feel Skye watching him, and when he glanced over at her, he caught a sense of curiosity in her eyes. None of the disdain he'd imagined people would look at him with when he admitted the lame reason he'd given up his racing career.

"That's pretty brave of you, you know—just to walk away at the peak of your career. Not many people can do that."

"It didn't feel like bravery."

They'd made it to the freeway entrance. Nico took the on-ramp and was immediately met by lane after lane crammed with cars creeping along at twenty-five miles per hour.

"Great," he muttered.

"So is that why you're going looking for Martin? Because you don't have anything else to do?"

Maybe.

"I've got other things to do. Finding Martin just happens to be next on my to-do list."

Although when it came to people to do, there was no denying the advantages of moving Skye to the top of his list. Getting on her good side—and in her bed— could mean finding out more than she might otherwise share with him about Martin's whereabouts. And if she didn't know where he was, that was fine, too.

Nico didn't need a practical reason to sleep with the star of all his recent fantasies. He might not have been able to trust her, but no way was that going to stop him finding out if she was as good in reality as she was in his dreams.

5

SKYE COULDN'T SHAKE THE feeling that Nico's intentions were anything but honorable. And if that was the case, she wasn't surprised. It only went along with her usual luck that when a studly prince type finally came riding up on his white horse—aka Ferrari—he wasn't there to rescue her. Rather, he had some other nefarious plan in mind.

Fortunately for Skye, she was no typical damsel in distress. If a gorgeous guy wanted to compromise her virtue, she wasn't going to let anything get in the way of her enjoying it.

Oh, how she could stand a little carefree enjoyment right now. Nico's presence in the car so close to her was an unwelcome reminder of her physical needs, which weren't exactly being met at the moment. A warm buzzing began between her legs, and she shifted in her seat.

Willing her thoughts away from sex, she watched out the window, where the Los Angeles suburbs seemed to spread out forever. She knew from having driven along the 210 before that the crowded-together towns eventually gave way to the low brush of the San Bernardino Forest, which led up the mountains to the vast brown Mojave Desert.

The rumble of the Ferrari's engine and the music on

the stereo made silence more comfortable than talking, and Skye was happy not to have to carry on any more small talk for a while.

By lunchtime, they'd made it into the desert to the town of Elroy, where fast-food signs advertised what seemed like their only chance for lunch.

"This is the town I saw on Martin's phone bill," Nico said, "so I thought we'd stop here first and look around, see what we can turn up."

"I have a hard time imagining the Martin I knew wanting to hang out in a little nowhere town like this."

"But the Martin we knew was just a lie. For all we know, he'd fit in perfectly here."

He took the next exit, and as they sat at a stop light, he said, "There's a pizza place. Want to grab lunch there?"

Skye shouldn't have been thinking of pizza again after last night's binge. "Um, okay," she of the non-existent willpower said.

The cool darkness of the restaurant was a stark contrast to the blinding hot desert sun. Skye peered out the window next to their booth at the town and tried to imagine living in this place, being a sun-parched desert dweller with no Nordstrom's within a hundred-mile radius. Scary stuff.

She gave a cursory glance at the plastic-coated menu, but she already knew she'd be game for any pizza Nico wanted.

"What's it going to be?" he asked after a minute.

"I'm easy," she said, shrugging and setting the menu aside.

One of his perfectly shaped eyebrows arched, and he gave her a look that was both amused and appraising. "Oh really?"

Skye caught the double meaning and felt that warm buzzing again.

"I mean, whatever pizza you like, let's order it. I like them all."

"How about a veggie pizza, then?"

"I wouldn't have pegged you as a vegetable pizza guy."

"Gotta watch my figure. I'm not as mobile as I used to be, and at the ripe old age of thirty-one, I've got geezer metabolism to contend with."

Skye smiled. "Do your injuries still hurt you?"

"Not really. It's just been a slow road to recovery, that's all."

They went to the counter to place their orders, got their drinks from the self-serve counter and brought them back to the table.

Sitting across from him, Skye found herself mesmerized by the rough, dark hint of stubble on Nico's jaw and the sensual curve of his lips. She imagined how that contrast of softness and roughness would feel against her mouth, against her breasts, against her thighs....

Whoa there, mama.

As Skye sipped her Diet Coke in a concerted effort to cool herself off, Nico asked, "How'd you get involved with Martin?"

Urgh. She'd managed to take her mind off her ex problems for all of a half hour, and now she had no desire to talk about it all with a guy as hot as Nico. She made a face.

"Come on," he said. "I just want to get the whole story. You never know what detail might help us find him."

"Okay, okay," she said, sighing. "It was a blind date, actually. We arranged to meet at a bar for drinks, so that if we didn't like each other, there'd be no agonizing

dinner to suffer through. There was a live band that
night, and we ended up dancing the night away. He was
a great dancer."

"Probably seemed like a smooth operator."

"That's exactly what he was, right?"

"You just had no idea how smooth at the time."

"Honestly, I thought there was something a little odd
about him at first, but I wrote it off as my usual bad instincts about men. We danced until the band stopped
playing, and then he asked me out for breakfast after the
club, and I said yes."

"Were you into him?"

She shrugged, almost embarrassed to admit the truth.
"Sadly, I was. I mean, he was handsome in that all-
American guy way, and he was articulate, and he
seemed successful. What was not to like?"

Nico's dark eyes had a way of projecting heat and
irony in the most disconcerting manner Skye had ever
witnessed. When he looked at her like that, she wanted
to bolt from the restaurant…or strip off her clothes. He
was the kind of guy she had no idea how to handle.
Should she go against her every instinct and trust him,
even flirt shamelessly with him? Or should she run like
hell from all the smoldering temptation he offered?

Skye recalled having seen him once on CNN, clutching a helmet under his arm and talking about some race
he'd just won. His dark wavy hair had clung to his
forehead in damp clumps, and while Skye couldn't have
cared less about racing, she'd stared, mesmerized by
him, unable to look away from one of the most outra-
geously gorgeous men she'd ever seen.

Later, when she'd met him in person as Martin's
landlord, he'd immediately lost his luster thanks to an

arrogant, aloof demeanor that she'd come to associate with every I'm-too-sexy-for-my-own-skin celebrity and celebrity athlete she'd ever seen in their off-duty hours.

"Hey, I fell for his act, too. At least you had some kind of instinct that he was scum."

"Perhaps the one and only time in my life I've had an instinct I shouldn't have ignored."

"So what happened when you went out to breakfast with him?"

"We ate pancakes, talked about our lives, laughed, drank coffee. We sat in the diner talking until the sun came up, and then he asked me if he could call me some time."

"So you didn't sleep with him?"

Skye blinked. "And that's any of your business how?"

"I'm just trying to get a clear picture of your relationship."

"Does this mean you trust me now?"

"No."

Skye bit her lip. She was the last person who'd be involved in Martin's con, but there was really no way to convince Nico of that. He'd just have to get to know her to see that she was trustworthy. Then again, she'd thought the same thing about Martin.

"It's really about as far from your business as we can get, but no, we didn't sleep together then. Or for that matter, the whole first month we were dating."

"Is that the norm for you?"

"Now you're really prying."

"Okay, okay. So were you suspicious of him taking things so slowly?"

"How do you know I wasn't the one insisting on taking things slowly? And since when did a month without sex become slow, anyway?"

A smile played on his lips, but he said nothing.

Sex. The subject hung in the air between them, and for the first time, Skye wondered if it was possible that Nico was as attracted to her as she was to him. No freaking way. It was crazy for her to be attracted to Nico…but if she was following the rule of opposites…didn't that mean…

It was all too damn confusing.

"Okay, if you must know," she said, "he claimed he wanted to take it slow, because he felt like there was—" she couldn't help but roll her eyes for this part "—something special between us, and he wanted to protect it and let it grow."

"Smooth," Nico said without sounding as though he meant it.

"At the time, it felt refreshing. And he acted like he was so interested in me, like he really cared about every little detail of my life. I'd never been treated like that."

He looked as though he was about to say something, but instead he took a swallow of his soft drink.

"It's a pretty awful feeling to have slept with someone so deceptive. And honestly, I was in love with him."

"He sure as hell was in love with you."

"No way. You don't lie to the people you love. And you don't steal their life savings from them either."

"Maybe you do if you're a con artist."

"I think his acting like he was crazy for me was all a part of his scam. There's no other explanation."

The scents of pizza dough and cooked cheese came wafting toward them, and Skye glanced in the direction of the smell to see a waitress bringing their pizza out. She'd gotten a sick feeling in her belly from talking about Martin, but in a matter of minutes, it would be obliterated by oozing cheese and a chewy dough.

"Why's it so hard for you to believe he really was crazy about you?"

The waitress placed their pizza on the table between them, gave them plates and served each of them a piece. "Anything else I can get for you?"

"No, thanks," Skye said to her, and the waitress left. To Nico she said, "Because I can't believe anything my instincts tell me, especially not about a guy whose whole life as I knew it was a lie."

"What's with you and the faulty instincts?" he asked, then took a huge bite of pizza.

"I don't want to talk about it." She turned her attention to her pizza and ignored his prying gaze.

If she tried to explain it, she'd sound crazy. And really, how could she explain that she'd never had a single stroke of good luck in relationships? That every choice she'd ever made had been the wrong one?

Who would even believe the truth about her love life before Martin: the high-school boyfriend who'd conspired to get hold of her panties only so he could string them up on the school flagpole on a dare, the college sweetheart who'd turned out to be a transvestite, the guy she'd, for a short while, thought might be The One until he tried to recruit her into his power-tool-selling pyramid scheme.

In each and every case, Skye had never had a clue about what was really going on until it was too late. She'd had no one but herself to thank for making such lousy choices in men.

But with her instincts telling her to keep quiet to Nico now, didn't that mean she had to spill all the sordid details? She was really starting to hate this stupid doing the opposite strategy.

So she told him. Everything. From the teenage horrors of her first date to the grown-up disasters and catastrophes that had made up her adult romantic life. By the time she'd worked her way to Martin, Nico looked incredulous, and Skye realized in the telling of it that she was even worse off than she'd imagined.

NICO HAD ALWAYS believed people generally got what they asked for in life. But Skye, on the surface at least, seemed like a normal woman. She didn't strike him as the type who went out subconsciously looking for jerks—who believed they deserved to be treated like crap in relationships.

But what other explanation was there for the bad luck she'd told him about over lunch?

After finishing their pizza, they went to the nearest gas station, filled up the gas tank, and bought a map of the town of Elroy. Nico had done an Internet search of the number that had appeared on Martin's phone bill, and it had produced the name Ana Zapata and the address 3844 Cortera Street. He'd considered calling the number and asking questions, but he figured they'd probably have a better chance of getting information if they showed up in person.

When they found the address, it seemed an even more unlikely haven for Martin than the town of Elroy itself.

"No way is Martin hiding out here," Skye said, echoing Nico's thoughts.

They both stared at the dilapidated little mint-green house with the chickens running around the dirt lot that made up the front yard, as if waiting for an answer to appear. Two houses down, some kids had stopped playing in the street to stare at Nico's car, and in the front window of the green house, someone pushed a curtain aside and peered out.

A few moments later, the door opened. "You looking for somebody?"

The woman talking to them with the hint of a Spanish accent was small and slight, her skin leathery and brown from the sun, her features sharp and hawkish. She wore her gray hair pulled back in a braid, and a faded house dress hung on her bony frame.

"Actually, we are. Are you Ana Zapata?"

The woman frowned and nodded. "Why?"

"Do you mind if we come in your yard and talk for a few minutes?" Nico asked, motioning to the short chain-link fence and gate that enclosed the yard.

"Sure, I guess."

Skye opened the gate, and they stepped inside quickly before any chickens could escape. They followed the sidewalk up to the front porch and stood at the bottom of the stairs. From this close to the house, the smell of chickens was overpowered by the scent of something good cooking inside.

"Do you happen to know a man who might be going by the name Martin Landry?"

"No, why?" She crossed her arms over her chest.

"He's a wanted con artist, and we're looking for him," Skye said. "We found your phone number on one of his old phone bills."

"How long ago was the call made?"

"About a month and a half ago."

"Could have been to talk to my no-good grandson, Julio."

"Is Julio here?"

"I kicked him out a month ago, haven't seen him since."

"Do you think he might still be in Elroy?"

Ana frowned again and shooed away a chicken that tried to get in the front door. "No telling where that boy is."

Nico felt his hope of this lead getting them anywhere sinking fast. "Do you mind if I ask why you kicked him out?"

"He was supposed to be saving up to buy himself a car, 'cause I was tired of loaning him mine. Next thing I know, he's gone and got himself a motorcycle I know he couldn't afford—the thing had to have been stolen."

Nico and Skye gave each other a look.

"What did the motorcycle look like?"

"It was black, real fancy-looking, had one of them BMW emblems on it. Not like anything you ever see around here, I'm telling you."

Hope rose in his chest again. "Do you know of anyone who might be able to tell us where Julio is now?"

"Him and his no-good friends hang out at that Spanish disco down on Main Street. But watch yourself in there. You're just as likely to get your wallet stolen as you are to find out anything about Julio."

They thanked Ana for her time, then drove to Main Street to check out the disco. For the first time since they'd left that morning, Nico had a real sense that they might be getting somewhere. But when they pulled up in front of the disco and saw the boarded-up door and the sign that read Closed on the front, he muttered a curse under his breath.

"Doesn't look like they'll be open for business to-night," Skye said. "What now?"

"There's got to be some other place around here that young people hang out. Maybe we ought to drive around and look for places Julio's crowd might go."

Next to the disco was a bowling alley. It seemed like as good a place as any to start, so Nico parked near the front door. "You ready to start looking?"

"Ready as I'll ever be," she said with a sigh.

6

AFTER A DAY of wandering the town of Elroy fruitlessly
looking for a guy named Julio with a stolen BMW motorcycle, Skye was starting to think maybe waitressing
at the Sunset Club wasn't such a bad fate after all. Could
it really be worse than this? Their search had been complicated by the fact that a motorcycle convention was
in town, as a part of its tour of Historic Route 66, and
every which way they looked, there were motorcycles.

Exhausted, they'd resigned themselves to staying
overnight here before driving on to Las Vegas in the
morning, but the cyclists had booked every hotel in
town. By the time they'd reached the seventh hotel,
they'd decided to give up and drive on to Vegas if there
were no openings.

But this place, the Budget Lodge, with its location on
the edge of town and its flickering neon sign reminiscent
of the kind of place where people checked in but never
checked out, apparently hadn't benefited from the arrival
of the motorcyclists' convention. The desk attendant had
assured them there were plenty of rooms available.

"No adjoining rooms," Skye said, having gotten a
little cranky after a day of Nico asking her the kind of
questions that implied she'd somehow gone out looking
for a scumbag like Martin to steal all her money.

"Fine," Nico said. And to the clerk, "We'd like rooms that aren't adjoining."

The greasy hotel attendant looked at Skye as if she'd just taken off her top and shaken her chest at him. "All righty. You can have 9A and 20B, so you'll be about as far apart as you can get."

"Perfect," Skye said, but not feeling so great now, with the lizard guy still eyeing her.

"I'll just need a credit card for the deposit."

Nico withdrew a card from his wallet and gave it to the attendant.

"This all gonna be on one card?"

"Yep," he said.

Skye felt a momentary pang of guilt for having Nico pick up every tab on the trip, but really, what choice did she have? She was broker than broke, about as hard up as one of her Cinderella heroines. And speaking of heroines, Skye hoped she could resist the lure of TV tonight and actually work on her manuscript for a little while. She'd brought her laptop on the trip to keep herself writing, and somehow, she was going to stay awake long enough to make use of it.

After getting their room keys—the old-fashioned kind complete with grungy-looking paper key chains— they went back to the car, grabbed their bags and scoped out their separate rooms.

"Looks like we really are pretty far apart," Nico said. "If you need anything, just give me a call, okay?"

"What time do you want to leave in the morning?"

"How's eight o'clock sound?"

"Early."

"Okay, princess, you pick the time."

"Fine, eight o'clock. And don't call me princess."

He headed for his room, but she could hear him mutter, "It suits you."

"I'm not going to say the name that suits *you*," she called after him, but he ignored her, and now that she was about to be alone in this dark parking lot, she hurried for her room.

Inside, she hit the light switch, which turned on a lamp on a table in front of the window. She surveyed her accommodations for the night, a vaguely shabby room that hadn't been redecorated in too long. Probably not since the mid-eighties, and the washes of mint green and peach on the walls and bedspread were too much.

Skye exhaled a ragged breath, carried her bags to the bed and dropped them, then opened the overnight bag to retrieve her cosmetics kit and pajamas.

Except, she hadn't really packed pajamas. The most practical thing she had was her little pink lace cami set, so that would have to do, unless she wanted to sleep in her street clothes.

She washed her face, moisturized, changed into the satin camisole and tap pants, then headed for the bed. She peeled back the horrid bedspread and was relieved to find a relatively new-looking blanket and sheets, thankfully white to keep from disguising any mystery stains. Then she powered up her laptop, inserted the disk with her work in progress on it, and settled back to get some serious work done.

If she was shooting for a minimum of fifty pages per week, that meant ten pages a day five days a week. Ten pages. She could do that tonight, couldn't she? She recalled seeing a coffeemaker in the motel lobby, which she could turn to for fuel if the pages didn't come easily.

But she hadn't written ten pages in one day in… way too long.

She had to find a way to get over this block. Really, her writing should be better now, honed by sorrow and experience, fueled by the desperation of unemployment. But as she read over the pages she'd written most recently—all two of them—she didn't exactly feel the words bursting to get out of her.

Sure, she'd written and rewritten the opening paragraph of the story fifty times, but that was the hard part. These middle pages of the third chapter should have been flowing out in an ecstatic first-draft frenzy.

Skye yawned, glanced at the little clock in the corner of her computer screen, and saw that it was ten-thirty. Plenty of time left to work, if she could just think of something, anything, to write.

She positioned her cursor at the end of the document, closed her eyes, and started typing. Maybe not looking at the crap she was writing would counteract writer's block. She wrote one paragraph, then two, then three, and opened her eyes again.

Did she dare to read it now? She scanned what she'd written. And it was garbage. After highlighting it all, she hit the delete key.

She leaned her head back against the headboard, let her eyes rest…for just a few seconds….

She was jolted away by knocking on the door. Skye's heart pounding from the shock, she set aside the computer and climbed out of bed, thinking it had to be Nico checking on her to make sure she was okay in her room.

"You could have just called," she said as she opened the door, stupidly forgetting in her sleep-addled daze that she should have peeked through the peephole first to see who was there.

Instead of Nico, she found the greasy lizard himself. His hotel attendant shirt gone now, replaced by a faded black T-shirt advertising Moe's Tavern. "I was just making sure the room's okay and all."

"Oh," she said, clutching the doorknob and hiding her barely clad self behind the door as she peered around it, prepared to slam it in his face if he did anything weird.

Out of the corner of her eye, she spotted the table-top lamp, which could double as a weapon if she got desperate.

"You, uh, need anything?" he asked.

"No, thanks."

"You know, there's pay-per-view on the TV. I could show you how to use it, if you're wondering."

"I'm familiar with how to work a television, thanks. I've used them before."

"Oh, right." His gaze revealed some dim, primitive intelligence, not unlike that of a reptile. "The pay-per-view's kind of different though. There's a special menu."

"That's okay. I've got work to do, so I won't be watching TV anyway."

"You some kind of traveling businesswoman?"

"I'm a writer," Skye said, proud of herself for not hedging. Whether she'd sold a book or not, she really was a writer. And if she never sold a book, she'd still be a real, live writer. No qualifiers necessary.

"Oh." He stared at her dumbly now.

"Well, thanks," she said, starting to close the door.

"You wouldn't be interested in going out for a drink or something, would you?" he asked, his tone turning a tiny bit pleading now.

Skye winced. How did she attract guys like this? She didn't want to hurt his feelings, but he was, with his pockmarked skin and dirty brown hair, truly one of the least attractive guys she'd seen in a while.

"Well, thank you, but…"

She'd never been good at turning guys down abruptly. Her instincts always told her to be nice, gentle, careful not to damage any egos. But if those were her faulty instincts talking, then what the hell did that mean? Slam the door in his face?

"I'm very busy. Sorry," she said, starting to close the door.

"There's porn," he said. "You know, the soft-core kind, on the pay-per-view. We don't have to go out no-where—"

Skye slammed the door hard and fumbled to lock it, her heart thudding even faster now, her stomach twisting at the thought of greasy-guy sex. Once she was sure the door was locked, it occurred to her that he had access to the master keys to all the rooms. Damn it.

She peeked out the window and saw him walking away, his shoulders slumped in defeat.

For now. Who knew whether he was really leaving, or just retreating to form a backup plan?

She couldn't stay here and sleep, not with the thought of him possibly returning later. But Nico had already paid for the room, and with the Motorcyclists of America in town taking up nearly every room, and with the way they'd gotten snarky with each other as the day and their fruitless search wore on, she'd feel horrible insisting they go somewhere else now.

She leaned against the door, contemplating what to do next.

Okay, so if she had no hope of switching hotels, maybe she should call the police and report this guy. Or call the front desk. Or swallow her pride and call Nico.

But she would not end up in Nico's room. No way, no how. She refused to let herself become a cliché.

However, wasn't it better to be a cliché than a victim in a police report?

Skye sighed and reluctantly left the door, then dragged a chair over to it and wedged it under the doorknob the way she'd seen done in the movies. She had no idea if it would do any good—probably not— but it made her feel productive.

Then she paced across the room, caught sight of herself in the dresser mirror in her little cami set, and debated over whether or not to change back into her street clothes, just in case she needed to bolt from the room in a hurry. Before she could decide, the phone rang, and she jumped at the sudden noise.

To answer or not to answer. If it was the greasy guy, she could hang up. She sat down on the edge of the bed, picked up the phone with a shaky hand and said, "Hello?"

"Hey." Nico's voice at this moment sounded both soothing and disturbing.

Soothing for its familiarity, and disturbing for the way it upset her equilibrium.

"Hey yourself. What's up?"

"I was going to ask you the same thing. Your room okay?"

"Aside from the creepy guy lurking around outside of it, sure."

"What? What guy?"

"That desk attendant who checked us in. Apparently

his shift ended, and he came by to inquire about my interest in an evening of him and pay-per-view porn."

Silence.

"You think I missed a big opportunity by turning him down?" Skye said, barely amused by her own joke.

More silence.

"Nico? Are you there?"

Then she heard the line click over to a beep-beep-beep sound, and she took the phone away from her ear, staring at it, puzzled. Had she just been hung up on?

The next thing she heard was pounding at her door, and, "Skye! Open up, it's Nico!"

She placed the receiver back on the phone cradle and went to the door. Once she'd pulled the chair away, she peered through the peephole this time, just to be safe, and saw Nico standing on the other side.

She opened it, and he took in the sight of her in her pj's, which she belatedly realized she was still wearing. Oops.

"You're okay," he said in an exhale of air.

"Yeah. You hung up on me," she said stupidly.

"I didn't see that scumbag anywhere on the way over here, but I want you to lock your door as soon as I'm gone. I'm going to look for him, and I'll let the front desk know he's been here harassing you. Call the police."

"Don't you think that's a little—" He turned and walked away before she could finish. "Drastic?"

Okay, so apparently, Nico Valletti was a mentally unstable human being. No other way to explain his sudden freak-out that she could think of. Just her luck that she finally thought she'd found a way to avoid crazy guys, and she immediately attracted two more of them into her life.

She closed and locked the door, put the chair back

under the doorknob, then paced across the room again, her brain trying to process Nico's behavior. Clearly, he wasn't the most normal guy around. And he'd told her to call the police. But it wasn't a crime for a man to proposition a woman, so what could the police do?

Or maybe he was right and she was wrong. Maybe this was another case of her instincts screwing her up. Damn it, she was getting more confused than she'd ever imagined possible.

She went to the bed and flopped down on it, staring forlornly at her laptop. The screen had gone dark but the CPU still hummed quietly, berating her for not having gotten any writing done. Well, now that she was wide awake, she might as well be productive, right?

She sat against the headboard again, brought the monitor out of low-power mode, and stared at the open document on the screen. *The Cinderella Solution* was the fourth manuscript Skye had started in the past three years, but it was turning out to be the hardest to write. Maybe that meant there was something wrong with the story, or maybe it meant she was suffering from growing pains as a writer, or maybe it just meant she sucked.

Her first two books had been flatly rejected by every publisher and agent on Earth—or at least in the English-speaking portions of it—but she refused to give up. Her third manuscript, *The Cinderella Factor*, the prequel to her current work in progress, was still making the rounds with a few agents, but she'd mostly given up hope on it, too. Which made the likelihood of her selling its sequel, *The Cinderella Solution*...a depressing thing to contemplate.

There was nothing she wanted more than to be a working writer, to earn a living from her novels, and somehow, some day, she would succeed. She hoped. She tried not to be doubtful, tried not to let negative thinking sabotage her, but it was hard when everyone in the business was telling her she sucked.

Maybe not in so many words, but she could read between the lines that said more civilized things like "over-inventoried at this time," "not to our taste" and "not a good fit for our publishing program."

There was another urgent knock at the door, and Skye jumped again, nearly sending her laptop skidding off her thighs and onto the floor. She caught it just in time, set it aside on the bed again, and got up.

At the door, she saw through the peephole that Nico was back, and she wasn't sure now why it hadn't occurred to her that he might reappear. Well, not any more than it had occurred to her that he'd show up in the first place.

She moved the chair again, jerked the door open, and glared at him. "What's the matter with you?"

His dark gaze traveled down the length of her and back up again, then he brushed past her into the room without speaking. He closed the door, locked it, then looked around the room as if he expected to find the desk attendant waiting to leap out from behind the bed.

"You're acting a little psycho, you know," Skye said, then immediately regretted it. If he really was psycho, he wouldn't appreciate her pointing it out.

"You should have called me as soon as that guy left. Why didn't you?"

She shrugged. "I don't know. I wasn't sure it was a big deal."

"Did you call the police?"

"What are they going to do? Arrest him for not washing his hair?"

Nico glared at her, but then the corner of his mouth twitched. "You're a real smart-ass."

She loved his mouth. Craved it, really. She'd have given up her life savings to know what it felt like to have his lips trace every inch of her body.

"It's part of my charm," she said, crossing her arms over her chest to disguise any possible nipple-hardening that might have occurred at her less-than-pure thoughts.

"So's that little tank top thing you're wearing. If that's what you wore to answer the door for the desk-clerk guy, it's no wonder he propositioned you."

"I thought it was you knocking on my door when I answered it the first time," she blurted, then realized her mistake a second too late.

"So you put that on for me?" he asked with a cocky smile.

"No, I just meant… Oh, forget it."

"Next time, use the peephole, and if it's a guy who's not me, don't answer."

"And if it is you, I'll be sure not to answer then, either," Skye said. "You can leave now."

"I'm not going anywhere."

"I can take care of myself," she said, though she did feel a zillion times safer with him there.

"I'm staying right here in this room, and so are you."

Bastard. Did he really think he could order her around? Well, technically, he could, unless she wanted to find her own way home from this little crap town with no cash and no ride.

"Okay, fine," she said as she dug through her bag and found a pair of shorts and a stretchy tank top.

"Don't change on account of me," he said, flopping onto the bed. "Hey, is this the book you're writing?

Can I read it?" He rolled to his side and turned the laptop so that he could better see the screen.

"No!" Skye dove across the bed, landed on top of Nico, and shielded the screen from his view with her hands.

She did not ever, under any circumstances, let people read her crappy rough drafts.

But now she found herself in the awkward position of being sprawled across a guy she barely knew, and she wasn't sure which was worse—trying to extract herself from the situation or letting him read her work.

"Don't you dare read that," she said as he tried to peer around her hands.

But then he caught her around the waist with one arm, rolled onto his back, and she was lying on top of him. With his other arm, he tugged her up so that they were nose to nose.

"You've just been looking for an excuse to get on top of me, haven't you?" he said, and she wasn't sure if he was joking or for real.

God, this was such a cliché.

"Let me up," she snapped, hoping her breath hadn't gone stale since she'd brushed her teeth last.

But now she was aware of all the hard places on his body, and there was a very distinct hard place pressing against her abdomen that couldn't be explained away as anything but a full-on boner.

And then there was his lush mouth. So close. So tempting she could hardly look.

"What's with you and the books? Don't you write them for other people to read?"

"It's a rough draft. Nobody reads my books until the final draft."

"Maybe I could offer you some pointers."

"Let me up." She squirmed, but he only held her tighter. "If I scream, someone's going to hear me and call the cops."

"But you won't."

She opened her mouth and screamed at the top of her lungs.

"Hey! Stop that!" He rolled then, holding on to her, and before she could wiggle away, she was trapped under him.

His solid weight pressed her into the bed, rendering her completely helpless.

"Is this the only way you can get any action? To force it?" she said as he pinned her arms over her head with his hands.

"You're the one who jumped me, babe. And while we're here, we might as well talk about a few things."

Skye knew she should have been maintaining some sense of outrage, but the truth was, all her outrage was draining away at an alarming rate, quickly being replaced by raging desire. Here she was, underneath the cutest guy she'd possibly ever been in bed with, and she wasn't so dumb that she couldn't recognize the potential advantages of the situation.

There was that, and the fact that she hadn't had any action since Martin.

"Here's the deal. I promise not to read your rough drafts, if you'll promise not to put yourself in any kind of danger while we're on this trip."

"I didn't put myself in danger. And why do you care so much, anyway?"

His lips went thin, and he stared at her for a moment. "There are a lot of scumbags out there, and you seem to have a track record for attracting them to you."

"I know you might find this hard to believe, but it's not by any effort on my part, trust me."

"I'm just saying, you've got to be careful. You're a beautiful girl. You catch men's eyes."

Skye blinked, at a loss for a smart-ass comeback to that one. Nico Valletti thought she was beautiful? She'd always considered herself decent—pretty, even, on those rare days when good hair, good skin and lack of bloating all occurred at the exact same time—but in a city like L.A., where appearances were everything and every other woman on the street looked ridiculously perfect, never once had she looked in the mirror and thought, *damn, I'm beautiful.*

But the idea that Nico thought so… Well, probably he was enough of a guy to call any halfway decent available female who was pinned beneath him beautiful.

"Thanks for being so concerned about my welfare and all, but really, it's not necessary."

"I'm concerned because I like you."

"You like me? I thought you were convinced I'm a con artist conspiring with my ex to rip you off."

"Maybe you are, but at the moment there's not much you could con me out of except my pants."

She was pretty sure a smart-ass comment was forming in her subconscious, working its way to the surface, but then he kissed her, and there were no more thoughts, snarky or otherwise.

There were only his lips, firm and hot, better than she'd imagined, and his tongue, tickling her mouth, coaxing it open, then stroking her from the inside. Crazy, whirling sensations formed in her belly and traveled to the aching spot between her legs where her girl parts met Nico's hard thigh.

Skye breathed him in, tasted him, and when he let go of her arms, she laced them around his waist, holding on for dear life to all his hardness and strength, feeling a little as though she was clinging to the back of a charging stallion. She had no control over where he went or what he did. She could only hang on for the ride.

She'd reached the place where she didn't have to make decisions—where her stupid instincts didn't matter anymore. The always-wrong voice in her head was drowned out by the hum of desperate desire that coursed through her now. All she could hear was the sound of wanting more.

Then he pulled back and looked at her with half-lidded eyes. His breath tickled her upper lip. "You want me, too, don't you?"

Well, *duh*. But she wasn't just going to give him the answer he wanted that easily.

"Maybe it's part of the big con you think I'm pulling. First I seduce you to gain your trust, then I take off with your car and your wallet. What do you think—is that how it's going to go down?"

"You tell me," he said. "Either way, I'm up for the seduction part, and I'm onto your game."

"Maybe that's part of my plan—to make you think I know you're onto me, so that you'll let down your guard."

"I'm the one who found you yesterday, not the other way around. I don't think you'd have a chance to plan out such an elaborate con overnight."

"Maybe I talked to Martin."

His eyebrows quirked. "Did you?"

She sighed. "Of course not."

"Then I guess I can trust you with my body."

"Do you always sleep with women you barely know?"

"Not always, but this is pretty much what I do with women. Or at least, this is what women like to do with me. You're no exception, right?"

Something about his gaze turned cold and flat, and Skye felt a little chill. "What do you mean?"

"Forget it. I didn't mean anything."

Before she could form any more coherent thoughts, he kissed her again, and as they kissed, he slid his hand down her side and under her tap pants. When his fingers found the edge of her panties and dipped beneath them, Skye knew they were at the point of no turning back. Either she stopped now, or there would be no stopping.

Her dumb instincts were screaming at her to stop, saying it was too soon, that she barely knew Nico and casual sex was always a bad idea. So that meant…she had to do the opposite?

Did doing the opposite apply to things that felt this crazy? Things that felt this good?

His fingers slid down her bare hip and around to her ass, and when he shifted his weight, his erection pressed into her where it counted most.

Damn straight the new rules applied here, she decided. She'd do it. She'd grab this night of pleasure, and to hell with her reservations.

For once in her life, Skye gave herself permission to do the wrong thing for all the right reasons.

7

NICO HADN'T INTENDED to be lying on top of this woman, in this bed, tonight. He'd come here to make sure she was safe. The thought of that jackass from the front desk harassing Skye had filled Nico with a fear he hadn't realized he was still capable of feeling.

Ever since he'd first laid eyes on Skye, she'd stirred emotions in him he'd thought he had lost somewhere along the way. He didn't really believe in love at first sight, but whatever she did to him, it was powerful. Maybe lust at first sight. Or obsession at first sight.

Obsession.

Such a strong word, but he had to admit, it kinda sorta fit. As he felt the smooth skin of her thigh, he wanted with every ounce of his being to feel the rest of her, to have her naked against him, wrapped around him, taking him in.

She brought to mind images of those old Calvin Klein cologne ads. He'd modeled for one, in the early days of his racing career. Some advertising person had spotted him on TV and called his agent, claiming Nico had the perfect look for the ad campaign. So he'd posed with some famous, stick-thin model he'd never heard of before, and for a while the ads had been famous.

But he'd never really gotten the emotion they'd attempted to capture until now. Until Skye.

The flimsy fabric of her little pajama set was hardly a barrier, but rather simply the wrapping for an irresistible gift. He kissed her neck and tugged down the silky shorts, leaving only her panties, which were purple lace. And then he couldn't help but stop for a moment to admire the way she looked in those panties, to savor the sight of her round hips, her long, firm legs, her dark-brown hair showing through the lace. He covered the purple triangle with his hand and felt her heat. Felt the dampness growing between her legs, applied a little pressure with his fingertips and watched her squirm.

She was beautiful in a way he rarely saw. She somehow managed to look sweet and seductive and sexual and completely different from any other woman he'd ever been with, all at once. She had the kind of beauty that didn't come from makeup or trips to the gym or plastic surgery or the most talented hairstylists. She was the raw material everyone looked for but few ever found—the kind of woman who in a different century would have been the subject of an oil painting.

"I want you," he heard himself whisper, not even sure what had prompted the words, or what they meant. Yeah, he wanted her physically, but he wanted more of her than that, too.

He wanted all of her.

"You've got me," she said, tugging the silky tank top over her head and tossing it aside.

Now she wore nothing but the panties, and when she opened her thighs wider, offered herself up to him, he expelled a ragged breath that sounded to his ears like a death rattle, as though the last of his will to be reserved and suspicious had just kicked the bucket.

He pushed her thighs all the way open and slid down,

trailing kisses over her chest to her high, round little breasts, which were a perfect, heavenly fit in his mouth. He sucked each nipple in turn, leaving them hard and erect, and then he moved lower, to the smooth, flat expanse of her belly.

And as he kissed, he tugged her panties down, freed her of them, so that when his hand slid up her inner thigh, he had full access to her.

Nico had been with a lifetime's worth of women, but none of them had felt this way. None of them had made him feel as if he'd found some secret treasure that belonged to no one but him.

He dipped his fingers between her lips, massaged her there where she was slick and wet, then slid them inside her, two and then three at a time, watching mesmerized as she closed her eyes and gasped at the sensation.

Resting between her legs now, he had an unhindered view of her pretty pink folds with his fingers moving in and out, in and out, creating a tight, crazy ache inside him that wouldn't be able to wait long for release.

Then he dipped his head down and drank in what he thirsted so badly for, ran his tongue gently over her clit, savored her soft scent, kissed and licked and toyed until her moans and gasps almost drove him out of his mind, and his cock, trapped inside his snug jeans, felt as if it might burst through his zipper.

She buried her fingers in his hair, tugging him against her as he coaxed her closer and closer to orgasm. He wanted her to come then, with his mouth against her and his fingers caressing her slick inner walls. And so he began a quicker rhythm against her clit with his tongue—quicker, quicker, until he could feel her contracting around his fingers, until she was squirming and crying out his name the way he'd imagined in one too many fantasies.

Somehow, he'd stepped into his hottest dream, and he wasn't going to take for granted a single second of it.

Nico kissed his way up Skye's belly and chest, then to her neck, and finally her mouth, still breathing a little fast. He pulled her against him, molded her body into his side and let her rest there with her head tucked beneath his chin. He was still fully dressed, but aching as if his bare cock was poised to enter her, and he wanted to savor the sensation.

"That was…amazing. Thanks," she whispered as she slid her hand under his shirt and up to his chest, where she caressed his nipples one at a time.

"My pleasure," he said, making the understatement of the year.

She smiled a little smile as she covered his body with hers. "Your pleasure is yet to come."

But Nico knew, if he didn't stay in control, he'd lose it way too fast and leave her with the impression that he didn't have an ounce of restraint, so as she straddled his hips, he sat up and caught her around the waist.

"Why don't you lie back and enjoy the ride?" she said.

"Because I want to be in the driver's seat. Old habits die hard."

It was true on the race track and off. If he didn't have control right here, right now, with this woman, there was no telling what kind of crash might occur. She was just too distracting, too tempting. He set her aside, stood up from the bed and undressed in a hurry, then found a condom in his wallet and donned it before returning to her.

Skye watched, her eyes still a little glazed from her

orgasm, her pretty legs folded under her. He climbed back onto the bed, his erection jutting toward her, but he would, no matter what, keep control. She came to him and pressed her body to him, then kissed him long and slow as her hands traveled over his ribs, around to his back, and down to his ass. She pulled him closer, and his cock pressed into her warm belly, but that wasn't nearly enough.

He tugged her with him until his back was supported by the headboard, and her legs were wrapped around his hips. Now he was poised against her hot, wet pussy, ready to enter. He held her hips still, then slid into her, all the way in until their bodies met and she let her head fall back in a soft gasp. He watched mesmerized as pleasure played across her features, softening her mouth, erasing the tension around her eyes.

He summoned every last bit of his willpower to focus on her and not the crazy-hot sensation coiling inside him, threatening to burst forth into Skye way, way too soon.

"You're so damn beautiful," he said in a rush of breath, and she opened her eyes, looking at him as if he'd said something in a foreign language.

She tried to rock her hips and quicken their rhythm, but he held her tighter until she stilled, and he slowed them down a bit more. Then he pulled her closer and took her breast into his mouth, sucking until she whimpered and gasped, then offered her other breast to him.

He let go of her hips and caressed her. The skin of her back felt like silk, so Nico focused on that and the sensation of her long hair tickling his hands as he held her. He let his fingers trail downward until he cupped her ass, which was both soft and firm, even sweeter in his hands than he'd imagined.

The thing about fantasies, he'd always believed, was that reality could never compete. It always disappointed, and he'd pretty much found that to be true.

Until now.

Until Skye, who was blowing his fantasies out of the water.

She started rocking her hips again, creating a dizzying friction against his cock, but this time he was powerless to resist. He could only move with her, kissing her with a hungry desperation as he edged closer to orgasm. Their bodies pumped faster, harder, and then Skye moaned into his mouth as she contracted around him, her second release bringing his first.

He felt a dam burst in him, felt himself spill into her in one hot rush of pleasure after another, until they were both gasping, breathing hard, holding each other tight in the aftershocks of their orgasms.

When they were still and quiet, he withdrew from her, disposed of the condom, and they stretched out together under the covers. Nico pulled Skye tight to him. Her leg draped over his, she rested her head on his chest and rested her hand over his half-erect cock.

In this position, they fell asleep, and Nico didn't wake until a few hours later. The lamp in the room was still on, and Skye's computer still hummed nearby on the other side of the bed. Amazing that it hadn't fallen to the floor during their sex.

Intending to turn the light off then return to bed, he eased himself away from Skye and climbed out, careful to cover her again. He moved the laptop to a nearby table, but the cord wouldn't reach, so he unplugged it, and somehow in the moving, the screen, which had been dark, came back on.

This was his chance to find out what secrets her computer held. If she'd had any contact with Martin in recent weeks, there might be evidence of it somewhere on the hard drive. He was no computer expert, but he knew how to poke around someone's e-mail and files.

On impulse, he switched off the lamplight, disconnected the laptop from its cord, and carried the computer into the bathroom and shut the door. With the light on in the little room, he put the lid down on the toilet and sat, then started exploring. The temptation was great to read Skye's mysterious work in progress that she was so adamant he not read. But no matter how sneaky what he was currently doing might have been, he couldn't betray her trust on that one issue she felt so strongly about.

But she hadn't said anything about not reading her e-mail. Okay, he knew that was shaky logic at best, but he wanted—no, needed—some kind of proof that she could be trusted, that his fantasies might be worth pursuing for more than just a night of great sex.

He opened her e-mail program and scanned the addresses and subject lines of all the messages in her inbox. Most of the addresses displayed the names of people who were probably her girlfriends and family, but a few were unrecognizable and warranted opening for further investigation.

Her inbox ultimately revealed nothing suspicious, so he moved on to her sent mail folder, which also proved free of e-mail that might have been directed to Martin, up until just before the date he'd skipped town. There, Nico found the typical messages he might have expected between a girlfriend and boyfriend.

Skye wrote to Martin in a tone he didn't recognize.

Nowhere was there a trace of her smart-ass attitude. Instead, she sounded sweet and affectionate, like a woman who genuinely loved the man she was writing to.

A pang of ridiculous jealousy stabbed Nico in the gut. He'd known she was into Martin, but seeing it here in their personal messages to one another brought it home to him in a whole new way.

One thing was clear though. Skye didn't seem like a woman who was conspiring with her man to pull a con. She seemed like a normal girlfriend, writing to her boy-friend about dates and lunches and trips to the beach and the typical hassles of work and life.

He found himself reading for the sake of his curios-ity after a while, and he wasn't sure how much time had passed when he heard a sound outside the door, and then a knock.

"Nico? Are you in there?" Skye called in a groggy voice through the door.

He looked from the door to the laptop and back to the door, his heart racing now.

"Yeah, I'm here," he said stupidly.

"Are you okay?"

"Yeah, I'm, uh, fine. Do you need the bathroom?" If she did, he was screwed. No way to explain sitting alone in the bathroom with her computer.

"No, I just got a little confused when I woke up and you weren't there."

He heard her footsteps padding across the carpet, away from the bathroom, and he breathed a sigh of relief. But now he'd have to wait until he was sure she'd fallen asleep again to leave the bathroom. Either that or leave the computer here, then try to get up again later

to move it to the other room. But before he had time to
make a decision, he heard Skye's footsteps coming
closer again.

"Nico, have you seen my laptop? It was on the bed
earlier, and now it's gone."

Damn it. Damn it, damn it, damn it.

Just then, as if to convict him, the computer's fan
kicked on, its low hum amplified by the hard surfaces
of the bathroom. He mouthed a curse and tried to cover
up the sound of the fan by flushing the toilet and turning
on the water faucet.

"No, um," he said. "I mean, I remember seeing it on
the bed. Did you check the floor? Maybe it fell down."

"What was that humming sound?" she said.

"The toilet?"

"No, that other sound. Do you have my computer in
there?"

The doorknob, which he'd thankfully locked, clicked
back and forth. But there was no denying that he'd been
busted. He could lie, concoct some crazy scheme, but
he might as well just admit what he'd done and get on
with her hating him.

SKYE STARED at the door, then back at the room she'd
just searched. Her heart raced at the thought of someone
having stolen her most prized possession, but much
more important were her files. All those countless hours
of work. Sure, she had backup copies of her writing on
disks, but she wasn't always very diligent about
updating her backups when she revised or added pages
to things.

But if Nico was sitting in the bathroom with her
computer in the middle of the night, what the hell was

he doing with it? Reading her work in progress? Looking for clues that she was a con artist?

"Nico? Answer me!"

She heard the lock click on the door, and then it opened. Holding the laptop on one arm, Nico stood there in his underwear looking vaguely guilty.

Skye took in the sight of him, her gaze darting from the computer to his face. "What the hell?"

She felt as if she'd been violated, but she didn't quite know how yet. Thank God she'd thought to put her cami set back on when she'd gotten up, or she'd have felt even stupider right now.

"I'm sorry. I just wanted to see if you'd been e-mailing Martin."

"You're playing detective on my personal computer, reading my private e-mail?"

"I need to know if I can trust you."

"You didn't seem too worried about trust a few hours ago," she said, but she was having a hard time staying angry.

Of course he needed to know if he could trust her. She had the same fears about him, and in similar circumstances, she might have done the same snooping.

He handed the computer to her, switched off the bathroom light, and brushed past her out of the bathroom. He strode across the room and sat in a chair.

"Do you hate me now?" he said, leaning forward and resting his elbows on his knees.

His short, dark hair was mussed, and in the dim light of the lamp she'd switched on a few minutes ago, he looked sublime. His olive skin, his sculpted muscles, his athletic cut black briefs…

Memories of their lovemaking assaulted her will to

be pissed off, and the only emotion she could muster was a sexually edged giddiness.

She couldn't remember the last time she'd had such hot sex.

She set the computer down on the dresser and put it on low power mode.

"So you read my private e-mail—is that all you read?"

"Yes, and I only read things that looked like they might be correspondence with Martin."

"Then you didn't find any evidence of me conspiring with him," she said, crossing her arms over her chest.

"No, I didn't."

"Do you trust me now?"

"I'd like to."

"But you can't."

He shrugged. "Not yet. For all I know, you're just smart enough to delete any incriminating e-mails."

"I still don't trust you either," Skye said, sounding more like a petulant teenager than a grown woman.

"Then I guess that makes us…even."

She didn't mean to laugh, but his vaguely amused expression coincided with her realization of what a bizarre turn her life had taken. This whole doing the opposite thing was leading her down paths she never could have imagined and never would have had the courage to take before.

"Are you laughing at me?" Nico asked, standing to close the distance between them.

"No, I'm laughing at us. What the hell are we doing?"

"Looking for Martin."

"It's the middle of the night in the crappiest town I've ever seen, in this awful hotel room, and you're Nico Valletti, world-famous ex-racecar driver."

He tilted her chin up with his thumb. "You're just now figuring out my name?"

"I mean, you're this hot celebrity, and I'm nobody."

"I'm a has-been, and you're the next big thing in the fiction world," he said, and whatever she might not have liked about him before, she suddenly couldn't remember.

He was brilliant and perfect and the sexiest guy she'd ever met.

"You're sweet," she whispered, right before he kissed her, long and slow and deep.

He trailed the kiss to her ear and whispered, "I have ulterior motives."

Skye's body warmed, then turned hot and liquid. She let him guide her back to the bed. He switched off the light and joined her, stripped off their clothes, grabbed a condom from the nightstand and slid it on. He tucked her body against his.

She melted into his warmth, felt his rigid erection pressing into her from behind, and arched toward him. He slid his hand over her hip and between her legs, where he guided himself into her, then kept his fingers there, working their magic on her as he pumped into her from behind. She relaxed into the slow, languid lovemaking, let drowsiness drift over her, and when she felt her orgasm coming on, it was almost as if in a dream.

As if she were in the midst of a hazy fantasy that was far too good to be real.

He bucked against her, cried out, and then she came, too, in a delicious wave of pleasure that brought her back to reality. She closed her eyes and gasped at the sensations coursing through her body.

This was real. This man, this place, this crazy adventure. And as Skye's body recovered, as she drifted off to sleep with Nico still inside her, she knew that finally, for the first time in her life, she was really living.

She'd gotten rid of all her baggage, all her bad judgment, and she was racing through life now, running red lights and careening towards destinations unknown.

Maybe she'd crash and burn. Or maybe…

Maybe she was finally living the life she was meant to live.

8

THE SCENT of coffee and fried things was strong in the air. Skye glanced around the International House of Pancakes and wondered where all the other people there were headed and how they'd ended up in the hellhole of Elroy at nine o'clock on a Saturday morning.

They were mostly retirees, plus a few families and a handful who looked as though they were in town for the motorcycle convention. Probably most of the retirees and families were on their way to or from Vegas, since this was the midpoint between there and L.A.

Skye and Nico stood out, didn't look as if they fit in the picture at all, really. Nico, especially, had an aura about him. Even if she hadn't recognized him from television, she'd be able to look at him and know that he was some kind of celebrity.

His perfect skin, perfect hair, perfect teeth and expensive clothes all spoke to the fact that he'd been groomed to be in the public eye, and his relaxed demeanor said that he was comfortable there. He didn't seem to notice the glances of the other customers, and when he did, he'd simply nod and smile as if he knew the person who was staring at him.

He never seemed bothered by the attention. And when a guy who'd clearly ridden in on a Harley and still had the bug splatters on his leather vest to show for it approached Nico and asked for his autograph, he responded as if he'd known the guy all his life.

Skye looked at Nico now with new eyes. He kept surprising her.

A tired-looking waitress finally showed up and took their orders, then hurried to another table to do the same. When she was gone, Nico smiled across the table at her.

"About last night," he said, and her stomach flip-flopped.

This was the part where he'd tell her it was all a big mistake, and from now on they'd have to keep their paws off of each other.

"Yes, about last night," she said. "I know what you're going to say, so I'll say it first. I'm sorry we kind of lost control. Probably we just needed to get that out of our systems, and it won't happen again."

He held up a hand to silence her. "That's not what I was going to say."

She blinked. "Oh."

"I was going to say, what happened was really…nice. I hope you don't regret it, because I don't."

"Oh." She was turning into a broken record.

"And I hope you don't mind if it happens again."

"Oh."

"I'd appreciate if you could say something besides 'oh.'"

"Ditto," she said, unable to form coherent sentences.

Nico wanted to sleep with her again. Last night had been rock-her-world amazing, and he wanted it to happen again. That wasn't so bad, was it? The problem was, she didn't know what her instincts were telling her to do anymore.

This is crazy, she finally heard the dumb voice in her head saying.

Which meant it wasn't crazy. Which meant she could screw Nico's brains out if she wanted to.

Yippee!

"All you can say is ditto?"

"I'm sorry. I'm just a little overwhelmed by all the stuff that's been happening. What I meant to say is, I'm all for more of what happened last night."

The waitress, whose nametag read Starla, returned, placing two large glasses of orange juice on the table.

"Here y'all go," she said. Some of Skye's sloshed out onto her napkin and silverware, but Starla didn't seem to notice and hurried away again.

Skye, having worked as a waitress for longer than she ever would have liked—and facing the prospect of returning to the profession—tried to be forgiving. It looked as if Starla was covering enough tables for three servers.

"You seem like you're brooding about something," Nico said.

Skye smiled and shrugged. "Sorry, just thinking about going back to my old waitressing job."

"Why would you do that?"

"To pay the bills."

"But you're a talented writer—"

"The talented part is up for debate, and I can't pay the bills as a writer any time soon. At least waitressing doesn't take any creative energy. I'll be able to write in the mornings and work serving tables at night. It'll be okay, I guess."

"Except you don't want to do it."

She shrugged. "Really, it's no big deal. Anything will be better than working at Dynasucks."

"Listen, I really am sorry about that. I never meant for you to lose your job because of me."

"Don't be sorry—it wasn't your fault. I had it coming. I was a terrible salesperson, and that job was sucking the soul out of me anyway."

"Then why were you working there?"

"Those pesky bills again," she said, gazing at the dingy salt and pepper shakers.

"My mother always told me, don't ever stay at a job that makes you miserable."

"Yeah, well, my mother always told me a great pair of heels can make any woman look beautiful."

Nico flashed a confused look at her. "What does that have to do with anything."

"It doesn't. My mother has always been full of useless advice."

"And your father?"

"Was the kind of guy who'd marry a woman who was full of useless advice. He always used to tell me, 'Marry a guy who has lots of money—then you'll be set for life.'"

Not that Skye meant any disrespect or anything. She loved her parents. But they had very, very limited parenting abilities.

"Where do your parents live?"

"They've got a house in Palm Desert now, but we lived in Huntington Beach when I was growing up."

"An O.C. girl."

She smiled. "Way before the O.C. was an in place to be."

"What are they like? Your parents, I mean."

"Imagine being raised by the disco king and queen of Orange County."

Nico expelled a little laugh.

"It's not funny. I mean, I guess they meant well, but they were just a couple of party people who probably never should have settled down and had a kid."

"So you must be a good dancer."

"I was a major disappointment to them when they discovered I had no natural rhythm. I can only dance well when I'm drunk."

"I'll remember that."

Skye smiled. She was exaggerating a little. She could dance okay, but she'd never be the queen of the dance floor her mother had been.

"My parents still dance competitively, only they've moved to the ballroom and salsa circuits. My mom still has a killer body, though she's had help recently from a few surgeons."

"That's probably the one thing I'll never get used to about L.A.—all the pretty plastic people. I mean, no offense to your mom, but it's kind of freakish."

Skye decided not to point out that Nico was one of those pretty people, but she didn't doubt that he came by his looks naturally.

"No offense taken. I'd love to see her age gracefully just so I could get an idea of what I'll look like at forty and beyond. But now all I've got an idea of is what I'll look like if I stretch my face to the sides like this." She held her hands to the sides of her face and pulled her skin back to demonstrate.

Caught in the middle of drinking, Nico sprayed orange juice across the table. He grabbed a napkin to clean up the mess. "Sorry," he said. "At least it didn't come out my nose."

"Sorry I made you spew," Skye said, oddly charmed

that a guy as hot as Nico could do something as goofy as laugh orange juice.

"You have any siblings?"

Skye shook her head. "Mom and Dad realized they were in way over their heads after they had me, and they both got fixed, just to be safe—a vasectomy *and* a tubal ligation."

"Wow, that's kind of like overkill."

"It was for the best. I mean, do we really need another screw-up like me around?"

"You're not a screw-up."

"I appreciate the sentiment, but really, I am. Do you have any idea how I decided to go on this trip with you?"

"You flipped a coin?"

"No, I'm doing the opposite of whatever my instincts tell me to do. It's a theory I'm testing out."

"Okay, I'm intrigued. Explain."

"Whatever I think I'm supposed to do, I have to do the opposite. It's designed to counteract my bad decision-making skills."

"That's…bizarre."

She shrugged. "Not really. I mean, if all my decisions have been bad ones, then the opposite has to be better, right?"

The waitress arrived with their food and set steaming plates of eggs, bacon and pancakes on the table. Skye normally wouldn't have ordered such a huge meal for breakfast, but after last night, she felt as if she needed the sustenance.

Nico began pouring syrup over his pancakes, then he cut them into little squares.

"Why do you think all your decisions are bad?" he asked.

"If I knew that, it wouldn't be happening."

Skye peered out the window next to them, her mind whirring around possibilities. Why was she such a dumb-ass when it came to men and most other life-altering decisions?

It was easy to sink into pop psychology excuses, like that it was her mother's fault, or her father's fault. They hadn't done much to equip her for the realities of life off the dance floor. But she was a grown woman, and she'd known since the age of seven that her parents were kind of useless.

That had been when she'd attempted to write her first book, a terribly angst-ridden story of a girl, her horse and an evil dog-food maker. Her mother had read the story, at Skye's request, and had declared that she should find something better to do with her time, like chasing boys.

Skye had confessed then that she wanted to be a writer when she grew up, and her mother had looked at her as if she was an alien. "Oh honey," she'd said. "Why don't you be an actress or a model or a TV newswoman?"

From that point on, Skye had understood the wide gulf between her mother and herself, and she'd rarely ever attempted to cross it again.

"Seems to me," Nico said as Skye dug into her scrambled eggs, "that you just need to be a little more confident. I think that smart-ass attitude of yours hides your insecurities. And God knows why you're insecure."

"Thanks for the analysis," she said sarcastically, proving his point. "What about your family? Where are they?"

He cocked an eyebrow at her abrupt change of subject, but mercifully went along. "Mostly in Chicago. That's where I grew up."

"Is your family Italian?"

He nodded. "Fresh off the boat. My mother and father grew up in Firenze, but they immigrated to the U.S. right after they got married, when my father was recruited to drive for an American racing team."

"So I guess Italian racecars and driving like a crazy person is in your blood."

He smiled. "Pretty much, though my accident has tamed me some."

"It must have been hard to lose your father so young."

Nico shrugged, and Skye sensed she'd moved into forbidden territory. She was curious to know more, but she supposed she'd have to wait.

"What about your name—Nico? Is that short for something?"

"Let's not go there," he said, then turned his attention back to his pancakes and took a big bite.

"What? Is it really that bad?"

He cast an evil stare at her. "Dominico. Dominico Giovanni Valletti."

She smiled. "I like the way you say that with the Italian accent, but you're right. Nico fits you better."

Her appetite crowded out her curiosity, and she attacked her eggs and bacon. She'd have all weekend to get to know Nico better, find out what made him tick, why he'd decided to become a racecar driver—but she only had right now to eat her breakfast before he polished off the rest of his pancakes.

Then something outside the window caught her eye. In the blinding desert sun, a motorcycle glinted as it drove by. But not just any motorcycle, and not just any driver. It was a black motorcycle with what looked like a little blue BMW emblem on the back—same as the bike Martin had stolen—with a guy on it who looked a hell of a lot like Martin. Skye strained to watch it as it disappeared down the street.

"What?" Nico said, watching her.

"I think I just saw Martin."

"No way."

"Seriously," she said, and the more she thought about it, the more she was sure it had been him. He'd been wearing a vintage blue plaid shirt she'd bought him for Christmas. The store where she'd bought it sold one-of-a-kind stuff.

"How sure are you?"

"Well, he was wearing a helmet, but he had on a shirt I recognize... Ninety-eight-point-six-percent sure?"

He gave her a look that said he didn't appreciate her humor, pulled out his wallet, and dropped a couple of bills on the table to cover their food and a tip.

"Let's go."

"But..." Skye looked forlornly at her breakfast, which she'd only gotten a few bites of.

"We'll eat after. We've got to move fast if we have any hope of catching up to him."

They hurried out of the restaurant to Nico's car, then raced out of the parking lot in the direction the motor-cycle had gone.

"Why would Martin be here?" Nico muttered.

"Maybe he's trying to sell your motorcycle, thinking if there's the convention in town, there will be lots of potential buyers."

"Possible—but what about Julio? Why would Martin have the motorcycle again if he'd already sold it to Julio?"

"I don't get it."

They drove toward the center of town, where frequent stoplights dwindled their chances of catching up to Martin or his look-alike. Skye strained to see down every street they passed and inspect every parking lot, but no luck. When they reached the town center, they had to choose between turning off toward the freeway or going straight toward who knew what.

"Try turning left," Skye said, and Nico skidded through a yellow light to make the turn.

Now they were headed uphill, passing more residences than businesses, and Skye tried to imagine snobby, finer-things-loving Martin staying in one of these modest houses. Impossible. She would have bet anything he was only in this town temporarily, that he was staying at a hotel and dying to get the hell out as soon as possible.

They got lucky with a couple of green lights, then found themselves nearing the on ramp to Highway 15.

"What the hell do we do now? We can go north, south or straight."

Skye was busy searching nearby parking lots, when she spotted the motorcycle and the blue plaid shirt pulling out of a gas station up ahead. It was an impossible stroke of good luck, one that had to have come from Nico's karma and not hers.

"There he is!" she shouted, pointing in the direction of the gas station.

They watched as the bike pulled out during a break in traffic, crossed the road, and took the on-ramp going north toward Las Vegas. Nico accelerated so fast Skye's head snapped against the headrest. And she held on tightly to the door handle as he cornered hard on the ramp, racing to catch up. The Ferrari's engine rumbled aggressively, and she suddenly felt confident that they'd catch up to the motorcycle, no problem.

"You're being a little conspicuous, you know," she said as Nico started getting close to the motorcycle.

"I don't want to lose the bastard."

"If he sees us, he's going to bolt, and if we get in a high-speed chase, someone could get hurt, or worse."

Nico let up on the gas. "You're right," he said. "I just wasn't expecting to stumble onto him like this, and I guess I'm not thinking straight."

There was an old gray pickup truck and a semi between Nico's car and Martin, but it was impossible to be inconspicuous in a Ferrari, and Skye's stomach sank when she saw Martin's head turn toward the left side mirror. He seemed to stare at them for a moment, and then he hunched down and accelerated so fast the bike left a big puff of smoke in its wake.

"Shit," they said simultaneously, giving Skye an unexpected pang of affection for Nico. Martin had never liked her potty mouth, and once he'd left her, she'd relished talking like a trucker.

Nico stepped on the gas, sending Skye's head slamming back again, then swerved around the trucks and took off after Martin. Skye opened her mouth to protest again, but then thought better of it. If her instincts were saying no, that meant she had to do the opposite, right?

She just had to shut up, hang on and hope like hell they could catch Martin without getting anyone killed in the process.

9

NICO HEARD the sound of sirens before he spotted the flashing blue lights behind him. Out of nowhere, an unmarked white police car had appeared, its lights and siren only now announcing its true identity.

He thought for a split second about trying to get close enough to Martin that the police would have to pull them both over, but as the motorcycle, which he knew well had been specially equipped with turbo boosters that made the Ferrari with its greater weight a weak match for it, retreated into the distance, he knew he'd lost this battle.

He pulled onto the shoulder of the highway, muttering curses as he did so.

The cop took his time about exiting the car and making his way to Skye's window. By the time he got there, Nico had his license and registration out, handing them over before the officer could ask.

"I'm sorry for speeding, sir," he said, "But that motorcycle I was following is stolen, and the guy on it is a wanted criminal. Is there any way you could call for someone to catch that guy and bring him in?"

The officer, a heavy blond man whose nametag read Luttrell, blinked at Nico, then inspected his license and registration.

A slow smile spread across his face. "It's an honor to meet you, Mr. Valletti." He leaned in and extended his hand.

Nico shook it, smiling carefully. He'd gotten pulled over his fair share of times for speeding, but he'd never gotten a ticket. Cops invariably took one look at his name and either asked for his autograph, or wanted to talk about his racing record.

"I'll put out a call for the nearest officers to keep an eye out for the motorcyclist," the officer said, then disappeared back to his vehicle.

He was on his radio for what seemed like a half hour before finally returning with Nico's license and registration, which he handed back. "Your record's clean, Mr. Valletti, so I'll let you off with a warning. Just try and be careful out there, okay?"

"Yes, sir," Nico said. "That motorcycle is mine, by the way, and the man on it stole a lot of money from me and my friend here. We'd really appreciate anything you can do to help catch him."

The officer looked from Skye to Nico and back again. "I'll be happy to do what I can. I'm heading north on 15, and I've put out a call to all available vehicles to keep an eye out here in town, and up ahead on the freeways, too. This highway splits up ahead, and 40 goes off toward Arizona."

"He could be headed anywhere, but we suspect he's moving toward Vegas," Nico said.

They told the police officer all the aliases they knew for Martin, gave a physical description, and he promised again to do what he could.

They watched the police officer walk back to his car, then Nico merged into traffic and paid careful attention to staying just below the speed limit. He kind of thought the whole notion of driving at sixty-five to stay safe was ridiculous, but he knew better than to argue the matter with a cop.

So many factors went into how accidents occurred, and most of them had to do with the skill of the driver much more than the speed at which he drove. Not that he liked that excuse when it came to his own career-ending accident, but he knew it had been a mistake in judgment that had sent him careening into the concrete wall.

"Do you think Martin would change his plans now that he knows we could be onto him?" Skye asked.

"We don't even know what the hell his plans are, and we have no way of being sure that was really Martin, but I guess he very well could. He doesn't have any idea what we know."

"I say we keep heading north for a while and see what we find. Maybe our luck will last and we'll find him again."

Nico nodded, keeping his eyes on the road. Skye's long legs were distracting, to say the least, even covered in a pair of snug-fitting jeans. She also wore a little pink halter top that made him want to bury his face in her chest, and a pair of pink sandals that laced up her ankles and showed off her sexy red-painted toes. Just having her in the car with him might qualify as reckless driving behavior.

She stared out the window, probably keeping a lookout for Martin.

Martin. The scum.

Nico had been trying hard not to let his anger at Martin consume him, but it was building inside, ready to burst out. He'd tried not to analyze why he'd become so fixated on tracking down the guy who'd stolen an arguably minor amount of cash and an insured motor-cycle from him, but now there was no avoiding the matter.

Martin had made Nico feel like a fool. In the fallout from his accident, he'd gotten mad at himself, and then he'd gotten depressed. Something inside him had changed, but he wasn't quite sure what. He only knew that it seemed a hell of a lot easier to be pissed off at Martin than it was to be pissed at himself for making the mistake of trusting him.

Then there was the matter of Skye. When Nico could have any woman he wanted, why did he want her so badly? And did he want her badly enough that he'd actually made up this excuse of hunting down Martin in order to get closer to her?

They drove for a while on 15, leaving behind the town of Elroy, and after a while, they came upon a des-olate-looking exit with a sign advertising the Sweet-water Ghost Town.

"Where's the ghost town?" Nico said, staring out at the empty desert.

"The map says it's up on one of those mountains over there." Skye pointed as she spoke. "You think it's worth stopping off and investigating?"

He shrugged. "It's not like we have any more appeal-ing options."

They exited and followed signs along the road that pointed toward the ghost town, looking for any hint of Martin or the motorcycle. Skye alternated between peering out the window and studying the map.

"It looks like we'll make a left up ahead, and we should be able to see the town."

They turned, and sure enough, in the distance, spelled

out in white on the rugged brown mountain side was the word *Sweetwater*. Nico didn't feel hopeful that they'd find anything more than a tourist trap, but he was all out of good ideas.

"You really think Martin would go to a ghost town?"

"No, but maybe he thinks we'd never look for him there, either, you know?"

"We need to make a right turn up ahead," she said, and a few minutes later they were on a narrow road winding up the mountain.

When they reached the gate to the ghost town, he asked the woman in the booth if anyone on a motorcycle had come through recently.

She shrugged, and Nico waited for her to elaborate. "I think there's been a couple of them."

"Any within the past half hour?"

"I just got back from a break. Other girl was here just left for hers."

Nico looked at Skye. "Any reason you still want to go in this place?"

She made a deer-caught-in-the-headlights face. "I don't know. I'm hungry. Is there food?"

"Sure is, hon," the lady said.

"Okay, we'll take two tickets."

They paid the entrance fee and followed more signs for the upper parking lot. Nico winced at the sound of gravel under his tires. He drove at a snail's pace, trying to make sure the tires didn't throw up any rocks that might hit the car. Ferraris were definitely not made to be driven off-road.

Up ahead, the town itself was built on the mountainside. Mostly the buildings were low-slung wooden ones that clustered and then became more sparse the farther up in elevation they went.

Nico parked, and they made their way across the parking lot, looking around for the black motorcycle.

"I guess he could have ditched the motorcycle in the desert," Skye said, not sounding at all convinced of her own idea.

The parking-lot search yielding no results, they gave up and wandered into the town. In the bright sun, they had to wear their shades, and even then, Nico could feel the sun burning through his shirt and knew he was in the kind of place where city slickers like him died quickly if they weren't equipped with modern conveniences.

Skye was looking at the brochure they'd been given at the entrance as they walked. "It says here we can take a ride on an antique train, visit a house made out of bottles, and explore the many shops the town has to offer."

"Hmm. Don't you think we should look around for Martin or his doppelganger first?"

"Actually, I think we should eat first. Looks like the closest restaurant is ahead on the left." She looked up from the brochure, squinting behind her little white-framed sunglasses, and froze.

"What?" Nico asked as he stopped beside her and looked in the same direction she was staring.

"I just saw a guy wearing Martin's plaid shirt go into that store over there."

"No freaking way. We couldn't be that lucky twice in one day."

"One of us should go in there. But the thing is, this guy had dark hair."

"Martin could have dyed his hair. And what if it really is him?"

Nico hadn't expected to find Martin so soon. He'd

imagined this all playing out differently—and later, after he'd had a chance to calculate the best way to approach Martin. Stumbling onto him in the middle of a tourist trap had not been on the agenda.

"I've got my cell phone—we can just call the police, I guess," Skye said.

"I'm going to go check it out," Nico said.

There had to be a hundred guys in plaid shirts wandering the desert today, so probably Skye had gotten it wrong.

"I'm going, too." And before he could stop her, she'd barged ahead and into the shop.

Nico followed and found her inside, peering around a postcard stand at a young guy with slicked-back hair covered in a hairnet, and wearing a plaid shirt. He was looking at a rack of handmade jewelry.

She stepped out from behind the postcard stand. "Excuse me," Skye said to the man. And when he looked up at her, she continued, "Where did you get that shirt?"

He looked at her as if she'd lost it. "I, uh, found it. Why?"

"Found it where?"

"What's this about?" he said, looking from Skye to Nico. He had a slight lisp and perfectly manicured hands.

"We're looking for the man that shirt originally belonged to—it's a vintage, one-of-a-kind shirt I bought for someone about a year ago."

His expression turned wary. "Look, I can't really talk. I gotta go now," he said, backing toward the door.

Then he turned and ran, and Nico took off after him. He chased him around to the back of the building, where there was a sharp drop-off with a gully below. When the guy in Martin's shirt realized he was cornered, he tried to bolt to the left, and Nico caught him by the arm, twisted it around behind his back, and pinned him to the wall of the building.

"What's the story?"

"Look, a friend of mine told me about this guy who had a BMW bike to sell real cheap, needed to unload it fast, so I tell my friend to give him my number."

"When was this?"

"I don't know. About a month ago, I guess."

"You bought the motorcycle from him?"

"Yeah. This shirt was inside the storage compartment. I thought it was a nice shirt, that's all, so I wore it."

People were staring at them as they passed, but so far, security hadn't shown up.

"That motorcycle you bought was stolen."

"I didn't know it, I swear."

Nico tightened his hold on the man's arm. "Where's the bike now?"

"I freaked when I thought a car was following me back in Elroy. I found some guys at a gas station, sold them the bike for two hundred bucks, and hitched a ride here."

"So if you didn't know it was stolen, why were you so freaked out?"

The guy frowned, trying to figure out how he'd given himself away so easily. "Damn it, man. I'm really sorry if that was your ride. I didn't mean no harm to nobody."

"Do you know anything about the man who sold it to you?"

"Not a thing. He showed up in town, gave me the bike and disappeared."

"How do I know you're not lying?"

"I don't have no reason to protect that guy. I don't even have the bike now."

"Did he tell you his name?"

The guy shook his head.

Nico let go of him. There wasn't any point in continuing. They'd clearly been chasing after the wrong guy.

"Get out of here, man. And stop buying stolen vehicles."

He took off running, and Nico turned to see Skye watching him with a stricken expression.

"We've got nothing, right?" she asked.

"Not a damn thing. He just bought the bike off Martin, it sounds like. Or maybe not even Martin—maybe somebody hired to sell it. He doesn't know anything."

She sighed. "I'm starving. Can we go eat now?"

10

"HOLY crap."

Skye stared at the traffic on the highway snaking through the desert and felt all her hopes of making it the rest of the way to Vegas today fade away.

"Either there's an accident up ahead, or we're caught in the weekend rush to Vegas."

"This is like the freaking road trip that won't end," Skye said as she got out the map again. "Maybe there's some kind of side road we can exit on and take for a while until the traffic clears up."

After their fruitless chase of the guy in Martin's shirt and lunch at the ghost town, Skye was feeling anything but optimistic.

"We'll get to Vegas tonight. I don't have any doubt. If we get up to speed again soon, we could be there in another two hours."

Unable to find a place where they could exit, she closed the map. "Looks like the freeway is our only option right now. We're stuck."

Skye found her phone in her purse and peered at the little screen on it, which told her she had three messages. She dialed her voice mail and listened to Fiona's voice telling her that the hot guy named John from Dynalux had stopped by to see if she was okay.

Next message—Fiona telling her that she'd decided to go out for drinks with that hot guy named John. Third message—Fiona, sounding a wee bit contrite, telling her to call ASAP because she and John had had a little sleepover party.

Skye blinked and hung up the phone. She tried to picture Fiona and John together, and oddly, she couldn't imagine why it hadn't occurred to her to introduce them sooner. Skye had gone out with John on a friendly basis countless times, and while she'd had various thoughts of asking him on a real date over the years, she'd been too worried about the idea of working with a guy she'd gotten romantic with to ever pursue the notion for real.

And she supposed that's why she'd never thought of matching up her two good friends. Some little part of her had wanted John for herself.

But now that she knew they'd hooked up on their own, she couldn't help but be happy. Fiona and John... John and Fiona... The more she thought about it, the more obvious it was that they could make a great match.

She dialed her home number, and Fiona picked up after a couple of rings. "Details," Skye said. "I want details!"

Fiona yawned. "Isn't it kind of early?"

Skye glanced at her watch. "It's after noon. If you're going to join the world of pharmaceutical sales, I think you're going to have to be introduced to the time of day called morning."

"Ha. Ha. It's Saturday. I won't be working weekends, okay?"

"Okay, okay, so what's with you and John?"

"Don't get too excited. We just had a little fun last night."

"A little fun? I'd be seriously surprised if there's anything little about John."

"Mmm. I really like him," Fiona said, sounding uncharacteristically dreamy.

"I should have introduced you two before."

"But you wanted to keep him all to yourself, right?"

"Not exactly. Well, maybe a little." Skye smiled, and from the driver's seat, Nico cast a curious look at her.

"We're supposed to go down to the Santa Monica Pier later today. I just want to know one thing though— is he a lousy actor?"

Skye had seen John's acting on a daily basis at Dynalux, where he slipped into whatever role he deemed appropriate—courteous salesperson, eager employee, et cetera—none of which betrayed his true personality, which was that of a funny, ironic and fiercely sexy guy who couldn't have cared less about selling Dynalux equipment. She'd also seen him practicing for auditions, and he'd never failed to impress her.

"He's a very talented actor. I think there just aren't an overwhelming number of roles for towering African-American men with dreadlocks down to their waist."

"Oh good. I was kind of worried that he was, you know…"

Skye knew. L.A. was bursting at the seams with wannabe actors who had no talent, but lots of desire. She and Fiona had stumbled upon more than their share of them on the dating scene, and there was always that awkward moment where you had to face either lying to your date, assuring him that yes, he really was the next Brad Pitt, or replying honestly and seeing an abrupt end to the fledgling relationship. For that reason, they generally tried to avoid dating actors.

Before she could reply though, the line went dead. She looked at her cell phone LCD and saw the little symbol in the upper right-hand corner that meant she had no signal.

"Lose your signal?" Nico asked.

Skye looked out the window at the vast brown landscape, made up of nothing but rugged mountains, dusty sagebrush and the occasional Joshua tree. "Yep, I guess the coyotes don't need cell towers."

She watched the screen until the symbol changed to indicate she was getting a signal again, and she redialed her home number.

"Hey," she said when Fiona answered. "Can you hear me?"

"Yeah. Where the hell are you, anyway?"

"We're inching through the desert on 15, stuck in the traffic jam from hell. Which is pretty much the story of our trip thus far."

"You haven't even made it to your destination yet?"

"Long story."

"Any luck with your Martin search?"

Skye sighed and filled her in on the details of their adventure thus far, carefully skirting the issue of her repeatedly falling into bed with Nico last night.

"So now you're headed to Vegas," Fiona asked when she'd finished.

"Yeah, I guess we're going to check out that lingerie shop, and then from there, who knows."

"Where will you be staying?"

"We've got a reservation at Caesar's Palace, but we might change hotels if it gets us closer to Martin."

"Except you have no idea if he's really in Vegas."

"Yeah." A weight settled on Skye's chest. She didn't

like to think about that part. She felt much more productive when she was focused on doing something—anything—to find him.

"So what are you going to do if you find him?"

"Good question…" Skye bit her lip, staring at the SUV in front of them. "I guess we'll figure that part out when we get to it."

"Don't be an idiot, okay? Martin very well could be dangerous—"

"Don't worry, mother hen. We'll call the police," Skye said, carefully leaving out the part about how she'd had a few daydreams about conning the con artist first, before getting the police involved.

"You promise you won't do anything stupid? No trying to con the con artist?"

Skye winced. Her no-lying-to-friends policy was being seriously tested. "Well…"

"Skye!"

"I want my money back. I need it back—you know that."

"Am I gonna have to come to Vegas and kick some sense into your ass?"

"Definitely not. Please, just don't worry about me. We'll be fine." Although she was tempted to beg Fiona to come straight there and keep her from doing anything stupider with Nico than she'd already done.

Probably what she needed more than a tag-along roommate was an impenetrable chastity belt. But even then, she had a feeling he'd find a way to penetrate it.

Or she'd find a way to let him.

This was all just her bad instincts doing the thinking again anyway, because really, what the hell was wrong with her getting her groove on with Nico?

"I want you to call me every day and tell me what's going on, okay?"

Skye had nearly used up all her minutes on the cell phone, but Nico would just have to pay hotel phone charges, she supposed. "Okay, I promise. Bright and early every morning, you'll get a full report."

"Very funny. No calls before noon."

"Don't you think you should start getting yourself accustomed to waking up early?"

"One thing at a time," Fiona said. "I've just made the decision to become a big sell-out. At least let me sleep in until my sleazy salesperson training starts."

"As a former sleazy salesperson, I take offense at that comment."

Nico glanced over at her with a puzzled expression.

"Speaking of salespeople, do you think John is serious about his Dynasucks career, or is he going to move on any time soon?"

"You'd have to ask him that," Skye said. "I know he doesn't get off on working there, but it pays the bills and gives him insurance so he can pursue his acting career."

"Okay," Fiona said, sounding distracted.

"What?"

"I don't know. I just have a hard time picturing him there, that's all."

"I have a hard time picturing you hawking pharmaceuticals. We all do what we've gotta do, right?"

"I'll have to get a whole new wardrobe for this job, won't I?"

"Yeah, the skimpy tank tops and patched-up jeans aren't going to cut it, but don't worry, I'll help you shop."

"If you're back in time."

Skye frowned at the idea. She'd never considered

that her little weekend escapade with Nico might turn into a long-term search. No, she couldn't let that happen. She had a life to get on with, and she didn't want to let hunting for Martin take it over. When she'd agreed to go, she'd never considered how long it might actually take to find him.

"I'll be back by Monday…I hope." Nico looked at her as though she'd lost her mind. "Or maybe not," she added.

"I'll let John know you're safe for now," Fiona said. "He's worried about you."

Skye smiled. "Thanks," she said, just as her phone went dead again. She decided not to try to call back.

It was nice to know she had friends at home worried about her, looking out for her. In place of a normal family, she'd pieced together her own ragtag family over the years, she realized now. They might not have looked like family, but they were even better than the real thing sometimes, because they were there when she needed them without being annoying as hell the way her traditional family could be.

Skye loved her parents, but they'd never understood her love of books or her snarky attitude, and she'd never understood their need to constantly be in the spotlight. Most of all though, she'd never understood why they'd decided being parents just wasn't a role they could handle gracefully. She hadn't been a bad kid, or even a slightly challenging one.

But she'd been like an alien life form to them, and when the going got tough, she knew the people she could really count on now were her friends.

"Line went dead again," she said by way of explanation to Nico as she dropped the phone back into her purse.

"Who was that?"

"My roommate, Fiona. She hooked up with John from my office—remember the guy in the cubicle across from mine?"

"Oh yeah, the big guy with the menacing look."

"He came over to check on me after my firing. I feel kind of dumb that I never thought of putting those two together before now."

"Much better if they meet on their own. People are just predisposed to being suspicious of blind dates, you know?"

"Remember—that's how Martin and I met."

Nico cast a glance at her. "You never said who introduced you."

"It was a woman who used to live in my apartment building. She's gone now, but she showed me how to make curtains for my bedroom on the condition that I do her a favor. And the favor was going on a date with Martin."

"That's kind of bizarre, don't you think?"

"At the time, I just thought she was being a really sweet friend to him. She claimed he was new in town and needed to meet people."

"Maybe she was in on his con."

"You think?" Skye said casually, but she suddenly felt like she needed to hurl. She eyed the side of the road, creeping by at less than a mile an hour, and decided she could make an easy exit if need be.

"It seems kind of odd, you know? She introduces you like that… How well did she know you? Well enough to know you had a savings account?"

Skye started gnawing on the inside of her cheek. God, she was an idiot. Why had she never made the connection before? The police had never even asked her how she'd met Martin. It seemed like such an obvious piece of the puzzle, and yet, everyone but Nico had overlooked it.

"Oh shit. Now that you mention it, she could have known that. Fiona used to have a hamster, and when we went on vacation to Mexico, we asked Susan to feed the hamster and water the plants. She could have found out anything and everything about us by rummaging through our stuff."

"Maybe she's like Martin's scout or something. She could have been helping him find his next victim."

In the distance, a Joshua tree's branches were silhouetted against the bright-blue sky like a bunch of crazy arms. Skye stared at the tree until her eyes went blurry, her brain racing around and around the idea that she'd been had so much earlier than she'd even realized, the idea that Martin could have had some other woman staking her out as his next easy mark.

The feeling of nausea swirled faster inside her, until her lunch started rising in her throat.

"Stop the car," she cried, covering her mouth as soon as she said it.

Nico screeched onto the shoulder of the highway. "Are you okay?" he asked as she scrambled out of the car.

And right there in front of him and the long line of traffic behind their car, she lost her lunch. It was the final humiliating straw in her Martin ordeal, and as Skye wiped off her mouth with a napkin from her pocket, she vowed it would be the last time she ever let Martin humiliate her.

Next time she saw him, she'd be out for revenge.

11

NICO FELT like crap. He hadn't meant to dredge up bad memories or upset Skye, but the deal with the ex-neighbor was something they had to explore. And either Skye was an amazing actress, or her reaction to learning she'd been set up by more than just Martin was another piece of evidence that she was only a victim like Nico.

A victim.

Damn it, he hated to think of himself that way. He felt like a fool, but he didn't believe in coloring the truth to make it look more appealing.

He wrapped Skye in his arms and held her as traffic crept past them. People in other cars, probably bored as hell by the monotonous desert landscape and the lack of anything better to do, stared at them as they passed. Nico turned Skye so that she wouldn't have to see them staring.

"I'm okay," she finally said, and he felt her stiffen against his chest.

He let go, found a bottle of water in the trunk for her to rinse her mouth with, and once she was done, they got back into the car. When Nico signaled to merge into the right lane, a semi truck left space for them to enter.

"You feel like talking a little more about…what happened?"

"Yeah, it's okay. I normally don't lose my lunch over stuff like this. I just… I don't know."

"Don't worry, I know it's my driving," he said, letting her off the hook. Whether he could trust her or not, he couldn't stand to see her get so upset again.

She laughed. "I'll be fine, I promise."

"What was this neighbor's full name?"

"Susan Tanner. But if she was involved with Martin, who knows if it's her real name?"

"Did she mention where she was moving to when she left your building?"

"She said she was moving closer to her family in Oklahoma so she could help take care of her sick mother."

Nico recalled the red lace bra he'd found in Martin's stuff. "Any chance she's a triple-D cup?"

He cast a glance at Skye and caught her puzzled expression. "She was definitely well-endowed, but she wasn't *that* big. I guess she could have gotten implants though."

"Maybe she did that after she moved away."

"But if she left town, then why would her bra show up in Martin's stuff?"

Nico shrugged, adjusting his hands on the black-leather steering wheel. "You got me."

He wasn't sure how much more of this traffic jam he could take. He folded the map out on the steering wheel and studied it. They were still at least seventy-five miles from the Nevada border. There was a little town coming up that probably had a few restaurants and gas stations—and would probably be overrun with people like them who wanted to wait out the traffic.

"Maybe she didn't leave town—maybe she just got away from me, but stuck around L.A. so she could be close to Martin."

"It's possible. The question remains—where is she now?"

"She could have gone on ahead of Martin to set up a place for him to live, or maybe stake out his next victim, if that's her usual job."

"Now we're just speculating. For all we know, he was conning her, too. We just don't have anything to go on."

Skye sighed. "You're right. But I should start making notes of all the leads and clues we have—all two or three of them. Maybe if we write everything down, it will start making sense."

She got a notepad and pen out of her purse and started writing.

"Good thinking," Nico said, just as the congestion began to let up a bit. He accelerated to twenty, then thirty miles an hour. It was the fastest they'd moved in hours.

In a matter of minutes, they were up to sixty-five, then seventy-five.

And just when Nico's spirits were really beginning to lift, just when he felt as though they were finally getting somewhere not only in the car but in their search for Martin, there was a loud, sharp thunk against the windshield. A moment later, he spotted the crack in the lower right-hand corner, which before his eyes turned into a shatter pattern that spread across half the windshield.

"Damn it!"

"Oh shit," Skye whispered, her gaze locked on the shattered windshield. "I don't think it's safe to drive like this."

"We can still make it to Vegas and have it fixed when we get there."

"Yeah, I guess you're right," she said, sounding doubtful.

Nico muttered a prayer that the windshield wouldn't

crack any further, but no sooner had the words formed on his lips than the damn shatter pattern spread. First to the bottom half of his side of the windshield, and then to the entire windshield.

He thought of a few choice words he wanted to spit out, but instead he bit his lip. Hard. And strained to see through the couple of inches of unshattered glass he had left to look through.

Skye fumbled with the map. "We're coming up on the exit to Calder. Only a mile or so to go, and hopefully there'll be a windshield repair place."

Nico decided not to point out that it was Saturday afternoon, and they could be stuck in yet another craphole of a desert town until Monday if their luck kept going the way it had so far.

With his few inches of usable windshield viewing area, he successfully navigated the car off the highway and to a gas station, where the attendant pointed them in the direction of Tito's Car Repair, apparently the only place in town that could replace windshields. Nico winced at the thought of letting some small-town yokel work on his car, but it wasn't as if he had a lot of choices at the moment.

From the passenger seat, Skye started giggling uncontrollably as they pulled into the large gravel lot in front of two squat brown buildings that comprised Tito's Car Repair.

"You think this is funny?"

Her giggles turned into a full-blown belly laugh, and she was wiping tears from her eyes. "Have you ever had so much bad luck?" she finally asked, once she'd recovered.

"I…" He hadn't, but then, somehow, now that he thought about it, this didn't really feel like such bad luck.

It felt like fate to be stuck in the middle of nowhere with Skye. In fact, all of a sudden, it felt a little like the best damn luck he'd ever had.

"I guess not," he said, though careful to avoid showing Skye how easily she could charm him.

On the door of Tito's Car Repair was an orange-and-black sign, faded from the sun, that read Closed. The hours posted on a dusty sign beside the door announced that on Saturdays the business closed at noon, and it didn't open at all on Sunday. Their next chance to beg for Tito's services looked to be Monday at nine in the morning.

"It looks like people live in that trailer behind these buildings."

Nico sighed and steered the car around to the rear of the car repair place, where a white aluminum-sided trailer looked as if it had been parked since sometime in the fifties. Bright flower-print curtains covered the windows, and someone had lovingly maintained a garden around the outside of the mobile home, complete with plastic whirly sunflowers and pink flamingos.

"Now what?" he said, strumming his fingers on the steering wheel.

"I should go knock on the door. If you go up, you might seem a little…intimidating."

"Maybe Tito's a racing fan."

"I'm pretty sure his wife isn't," Skye said, but before Nico could point out that a lot of women whose names were not Skye Ellison loved racing, the door of the trailer opened.

A thick man with leathery brown skin and a head full of black hair stood in the doorway, his gray overalls stained from a day in the garage. "Sorry, we're closed!" he called out.

Nico lowered the passenger window, and Skye smiled and waved. "I hate to bother you," she said. "But we've got a broken windshield and desperately need to have it fixed. Are you Tito?"

The man shook his head. "No, I'm his brother. I don't know how to fix windshields, sorry."

"But the guy at the gas station said you do windshield repair here."

"Yeah, we do," the man said, a Spanish lilt in his words. "But Tito does that. He's gone to Laughlin for the weekend. Won't be back till Monday."

Nico was beyond getting pissed off. "Is there anyone else in town who replaces windshields?"

The man shook his head. "Sorry. You come back Monday morning, first thing, Tito'll fix you up."

"Won't you need to special order a windshield to fit the car?" Nico asked.

The man frowned. "Yeah, I guess you're right. You write down the make and model, and I'll call our supplier now. We can probably have the part up here by Monday if you got the cash to pay."

Nico nodded, taking Skye's notepad and pen to write down the car information. He got out of the car and walked the paper to the front steps of the trailer, then handed it to Tito's brother.

"Whatever it costs to get a windshield up here by Monday morning, doesn't matter. I really appreciate you doing the special order now."

"No problem, man."

When he was back in the car, Skye cast an exasperated look at him, then smiled. "I guess we're stuck here."

"Are there any hotels around here?" Nico called out the window.

The man pointed to the southwest. "Other side of the highway, Jenny's Roadside Motel."

"Thanks!" Skye said as they pulled away. "We'll be back Monday morning."

Five minutes later, they'd found their way to a dilapidated pink stucco building that stretched out in a two-story row of motel rooms. The vintage neon sign advertised Jenny's Roadside Motel as having thirty clean rooms with cable TV.

The ultimate in roadside luxury.

"Wow," Skye said, sounding anything but impressed. "I guess we're, um, here."

"I'll go get us a couple of rooms," he said as he opened the car door.

She laughed. "After our last hotel experience, I'm thinking one room with two beds will be plenty."

This was the part where he should have protested, should have said they'd be better off keeping a little distance, but no way in hell could he speak the words. He'd gone off on this crazy road trip and left his common sense back in Malibu, possibly never to be heard from again.

As long as Skye was his for the taking, there wouldn't be any use in trying to practice restraint.

SKYE THUMBED through the brochures she'd collected in the motel lobby, all advertising the many tourist attractions the desert had to offer. If they had to stay here in Calder, California, until Monday, surely they could find some interesting way to entertain themselves.

Nico emerged from the bathroom, having just taken a shower, and Skye stared in awe at the sight of him all damp and flushed, with a skimpy white towel wrapped around his waist.

Or maybe they wouldn't need to leave the hotel room at all.

"Watch out for the light fixture over the bathtub. It's a bare bulb dangling from a wire that looks like someone's five-year-old did the installation."

This was the point where Skye was supposed to make some witty reply, but instead she just stared, aware that her jaw was gaping slightly. Had there ever been a man as gorgeous as Nico on earth—or in her bed?

He headed for his bag, but stopped next to her and glared at the brochures. "You find any interesting tourist attractions?"

"With a mere five-hour drive, we can be at any one of a number of fascinating destinations."

"Hmm."

"There's actually one option we don't need a car for. One of the main roads into Death Valley starts here in Calder, and a tour bus leaves every morning at eight, goes up the valley and returns at night."

Nico shrugged. "I've always wanted to see Death Valley."

"It's not exactly getting us any closer to Martin, but—"

"But what else are we going to do?"

"We could spend tonight asking around town about Martin, but without any names or pictures to go by, I don't think we're going to get very far."

Nico was staring at her now instead of the brochure, and something about his gaze made her feel as though she was the one who was nearly naked instead of him. "You're feeling all better?" he asked.

"Oh yeah," she said, embarrassed to discuss her roadside puke now. "One hundred percent better. I'm sorry about your car's windshield."

"Could be worse," he said, taking her hand and pulling her to a standing position.

Now that she stood next to him, she felt the sheer force of their attraction taking over. There would be no acting sensibly, not with Nico and his skimpy towel within arm's reach.

"Thanks for taking the initiative to go after Martin," she said, not sure where the feelings of gratitude were coming from. "I never could have done this on my own."

"We'll get him one way or another, but I don't want to talk about Martin right now."

He pulled her against him, encircled her waist with his hands, and she melted into him. Definitely not the time to be thinking of her scumbag ex, what's-his-name.

"What are you doing?" Skye murmured against Nico's chest as he held her.

"I can't stop wanting you, but..."

She trailed her hands from his hot chest up to his neck, then traced her fingers around the soft skin there until they were buried in his wet hair.

"But you're not sure how much you can trust me," she said.

He said nothing, but she could see the answer in his eyes, and for the first time, she realized the power she had over him. Crazy as it seemed, she could see that he had no control over his desire for her.

He, of all the men on earth, saw something in her that she didn't see. Some powerful sexuality that only he had brought out. And she liked it.

But just as much as he feared he couldn't trust her

completely, she should have had the same wariness. She didn't know this man, didn't know what he was capable of or how he himself might have been involved in Martin's deception.

No, that was just fear talking. She was panicking— that's all. Everything was too crazy, too confusing, too much to contemplate when all she wanted was to get lost in Nico's arms.

He backed her up against the dresser, and when she brushed against his towel, it fell to the floor, exposing his naked body and his jutting erection. Skye's gaze dropped below his waist and lingered there until he lifted her onto the dresser and pressed himself between her legs.

"Should I be afraid?" he whispered in her ear.

In any other situation, the question would have been laughable. Afraid? Of Skye? Ridiculous.

But the way he made her feel, like a purely sexual being, worthy of his desire, made her wonder. Could they get lost in this affair? Could they lose their mission, their purpose, the drive to get revenge?

Be afraid, be very afraid.

Maybe it didn't matter if they could ultimately trust each other or not. Maybe all that mattered was what they could do for each other. Maybe, Skye realized then, it was to her advantage to keep Nico on edge, unsure if she could be trusted.

Maybe that's the only power she had.

For now, that's what she would do.

"You'll have to find out for yourself," she said, watching his reaction.

His gaze turned hard.

"Is that a challenge?"

His erection pressed against her jeans, and his large hands held her hips firmly, possessively.

"Maybe," she said.

Across the room, the picture window's curtains were wide open, and anyone who passed by could see directly in. Skye thought of pointing out their exposure to Nico, but then he kissed her, and she couldn't speak. His tongue toyed with hers as he freed her of her jeans and panties, then he broke the kiss to remove her top.

She cast one more glance at the window, which faced the parking lot, and realized their exposure only made the situation more exciting. She loved the danger of possibly being caught.

Nico's wallet lay on the dresser next to them, and he removed another condom from it—the man seemed to have an endless supply. He must have been a pro at playing women, and for once, Skye wanted to be played. She wanted this tawdry, no-strings-attached, no-chance-of-a-future weekend.

Skye, with her bad instincts and her lousy track record with men, finally felt confident that she wasn't making any wrong turns. She was forging straight ahead, wanting nothing more than great sex, and getting it.

Getting it good.

Leaning back on her arms, she propped her legs up on the dresser, on either side of Nico, and opened herself up to him. He rubbed the head of his cock against her, creating a greater and greater need in her until she wanted to impale herself on him.

When she didn't think she could take another second of the torture, he pushed himself into her in one slow thrust, opening her up, watching her expression as he did so. She stretched and burned around him, and then as he began to move within her, the discomfort settled into a delicious tightness.

Like a hunger that was finally being fed.

She watched where their bodies met, connected and moving together, and then she looked up to see him looking at her with dark eyes glazed with desire. Her breath, coming fast and shallow, caught in her throat at the intensity of his expression.

He slid his fingers down her belly, through her pubic hair, and against her clit, rubbing gently. But she was already so aroused, it only took that light sensation to push her unexpectedly over the edge. The sweet tightness turned into delicious waves of pleasure, rocking her body against him. She arched her back, cried out, helpless but to ride the waves he sent careening through her. And as he stilled himself inside her, giving her time to recover, she caught her breath and looked into his eyes again.

Out of the corner of her eye, she caught some motion, and she looked over to see a couple passing by just as they glanced into the window and saw her and Nico locked together.

"Oops," she whispered.

Nico glanced at the window, and the couple looked embarrassed and moved on. "Why didn't you tell me we had an audience?"

"They just showed up," she said, smiling and feeling a tiny bit ridiculous.

It was really only the danger of getting caught that was a turn-on—not the actual getting caught part, she realized now as her face burned.

"We'd better close those curtains before we get

arrested or the whole town shows up to watch," he said, easing out of her.

"Yeah, there doesn't seem to be much in the way of entertainment around here." Skye coveted his bare, perfectly sculpted ass as he walked across the room.

As he drew the curtains closed, she slid her hands down the hard planes of his back and over the smooth skin of his backside, savoring the warm feel of him.

"You have an amazing body," she said, and he froze against her touch, standing next to the small table and chairs that sat in front of the window.

She slid her hands around his hips. One made its way along the bulging muscle of his thigh, while the other gripped his erection and massaged gently. Nico expelled a ragged breath, then turned impatiently and caught her in his arms again.

"Now that we've got a little privacy, let's finish what we started."

He turned her around and steadied her against the table, then pressed his cock into her from behind. Skye cried out at the jolt of sensation, and as he pumped into her, his fingers teasing her nipples, he leaned against her and sank his teeth gently into her neck.

His bite sent chills through her, heightening every other sensation she felt. His breath came out hard and fast against her neck, and he made his claim on her, driving into her harder and faster until she wondered idly if the table might give way beneath them. As she heard the groan of the wood straining, Skye felt another orgasm overtaking her.

She contracted around him, crying out loudly enough for anyone in neighboring rooms to hear, and on the crest of her orgasm came his. She felt the strength of his release course through her as he pounded into her those last few times, his moans of pleasure next to her ear now drowning out all other sound.

After a moment of stillness, he eased out of her again, just as one leg of the table gave way and it collapsed beneath her. Nico caught her before she could fall with it, then lifted her and carried her to the bed, where they stretched out on top of the covers together, laughing.

"Public indecency, broken furniture—if we're not careful, we're going to get kicked out of this place," she said. And the way their luck had gone, it wouldn't have surprised her in the least.

Nico smiled and closed his eyes. Skye wiped the film of sweat off his forehead with her fingertips. Her heart rate returned to normal as she lay against him, his arm draped across her belly. She stared up at the popcorn-textured ceiling and the circa-1960 light fixture, her brain trying to take in what had just happened.

It was as if all their doubts about each other had been embodied in that one sex act. Their tension and their desire—all mixed up and confused.

She'd never experienced sex with such an edge before, and she had to admit, she liked it.

No.

Loved it.

She loved this newfound sense of her sexuality that had nothing to do with her stupid decisions or her bad instincts—had only to do with wanting a man and having him physically.

It was hot. And empowering.

"That was kind of crazy," Nico said, his voice soft as if he wasn't sure whether she was asleep or awake.

She glanced over at him and caught the amusement in his eyes. "A good kind of crazy," she said.

"You're like an addiction, you know that?"

Her, an addiction. It sounded insane, but she knew what he meant. The sexual chemistry between them was irresistible, and maybe dangerous if they weren't careful to take it for just what it was.

They were fulfilling a physical need like hunger or thirst—that was all.

"Did you get your fix?"

"For now. We should go have dinner, don't you think?"

Skye sighed at the thought of the culinary possibilities. The town was full of nothing but fast-food restaurants and greasy spoon places that catered to truckers and traveling retirees.

She was going to need heart bypass surgery after this trip.

"Do we have to?"

"I could eat you all night, but I think you'll start getting hungry after a while."

Skye tried not to smile. "Point taken."

She pried herself away from her comfortable spot next to Nico and went to the bathroom, took a quick shower and dressed. Out of the blue, it occurred to her how far she'd come from being Martin's hapless victim.

And, she was thrilled to realize, too, she didn't give a damn one way or another about him any more. For the first time since he'd disappeared from her life, the thought of Martin didn't arouse any sort of emotion—positive or negative.

Maybe doing the opposite, crazy as it sounded, was going to work out after all.

12

THE SKY in the desert seemed to be a window to a different universe than what could be seen in L.A. Even on a relatively low-smog night, the L.A. skyline revealed little except an inky blackness. But here, Nico could see more stars than he'd ever seen in his life.

"Amazing, isn't it?" Skye said as she sat down on the blanket next to him.

They'd decided to skip eating inside yet another seedy restaurant or fast-food joint, and the thought of returning to their crappy hotel room had held little appeal. So after spotting the hotel's pool, which was officially closed for the night, they'd opted to grab a blanket from their room, hop the fence to the pool, and sit waterside to eat their paper-wrapped tacos.

Nico had felt on edge ever since their encounter in the hotel room. He'd never had sex with a woman that way—so aggressively, so intensely. Their physical relationship had an edge like nothing he'd ever felt before. Something dangerous and a little out of control.

Something out of his most erotic fantasies.

His cock stirred just thinking about it again.

"What's up?" Skye asked as she tried to reconstruct her taco that had just fallen apart after one bite.

Nico, trying not to smile at her unintended pun, shrugged and sipped his Coke. "Nothing."

"Have you ever been to the desert before?"

"Just driving through to Vegas. I've never had an entire weekend to be stuck here."

"I love the nighttime here. I mean, where my parents live in Palm Desert is quite a bit different from this place at the edge of civilization, but at night everything looks the same."

"All this vast darkness."

He ate the rest of his taco in a few bites, aware that Skye was watching him now.

"Do you ever miss racing?" she asked, and his stomach tightened.

Good question. He shrugged. "I try not to miss things I can't have."

"Couldn't you still go back to it? I mean, if you wanted to?"

He felt a little twinge of annoyance at the question, but when he looked at her, he saw nothing but openness and curiosity in her expression.

"I had that choice, but I opted for retirement. I've always thought I'd only get one big crash to walk away from, and after that all my luck would be used up."

"That doesn't make any sense. I mean, if it's what you love to do—"

"The luck thing's just an excuse," he blurted, suddenly aware that he wanted to tell her the whole truth.

"Then what's the truth?"

He watched moonlight glinting off the pool water, and in a rush, he recalled what he could of the crash, the burning, the pain. Part of his physical therapy had involved water exercise and therapy. He'd felt like a failure during his long recovery, like a washed-up has-been.

But now he knew he'd just gotten spoiled by the lime-light and that he was lucky to have had his racing career, regardless of how or when it had ended. He was lucky to have lived.

"The truth is, I didn't want to go back. It seemed like I'd done all I could do as a driver, and anything else was going to be…I don't know. Redundant, I guess."

"Sounds like you're ready for a new challenge."

"Maybe, but I don't have a clue what it is."

Skye took another bite of her taco, and it fell apart again. Once she'd pieced it back together, she said, "I can help you figure out what your next career will be. I'm pretty good at that."

He cast a suspicious look at her. "I thought you were a writer, not a guidance counselor."

"As a writer, I like figuring out what makes people tick, what motivates them, what interests them."

"So you're a people watcher."

She nodded. "And an excellent listener."

"If you can figure out what the next big thing is for a washed-up racecar driver, you'll have my undying gratitude."

"I can think of other things I'd rather have," she said, a dirty little smile playing on her lips.

He loved the way she had of saying the unexpected. She made him feel the same kind of rush he'd experienced on the track, when he'd gotten into the perfect groove and he knew the finish line was his. No woman had ever made him feel that way.

He hadn't even realized it was a feeling that could be experienced off the track until now. But if he became addicted to Skye the way he'd become addicted to racing, would he ultimately crash and burn again? And this time, would it be a crash he could recover from?

"Whatever you want, you've got it."

Skye's eyes sparkled in the light reflected off the pool water. "I guess the question at hand is, what do you want? Haven't you been doing promotional stuff lately?"

"Yeah, I've done some commercials and endorsements, but that work's drying up fast the farther I get from my departure from racing."

"Is that what you want to do?"

He shrugged. "It pays the bills." And left a hollow feeling in his gut.

"Did you ever have a backup plan? Something you wanted to do if you couldn't be a racecar driver?"

"Sort of like your backup plan to work crap jobs while you wait for your writing career to take off?"

Skye gave him a look. "Not funny. I'm the one trying to help you here."

"Sorry. I didn't mean it that way. I just meant, you know, when you have a dream, you don't really want to think of not achieving it."

"I know all too well." She unwrapped a second taco and bit into it, this time managing to keep it intact.

"Really, no, I never thought I wouldn't make it as a driver."

"So you need to find your next dream."

"I've thought about opening a fantasy racing camp for amateurs who want to pretend they're racing pros for the weekend. I've got the contacts and the cash, and I think there's a demand for it."

"So what's holding you back?"

"I don't know. It's hard to explain."

Nico felt a little stirring inside himself, a familiar feeling that had nagged at him recently. The idea that he should be doing something important now that he had the money and the celebrity to put behind it. But what? He felt like a cliché to admit the first thing that came to mind.

Skye was watching him. "What?" she said. "You're thinking about something."

"It sounds stupid, but I feel like I should be helping people or something—maybe start some kind of charity organization."

She smiled. "That doesn't sound stupid at all. It sounds perfect. You could tie the charity to the sports camp, so that a portion of the proceeds go to your charity, and that would probably be an additional draw for business—so people could feel like they're having fun but still contributing to a good cause."

He nodded, thinking hard about her idea. It could work. For the first time since his last race, a feeling of synergy descended on him like a gift from above. He'd thought it was gone for good—that he might never have that sense of rightness and purpose again. But maybe… Maybe Skye had helped him figure out his next move.

He heard voices coming from the parking lot next to the pool, and they looked over to see the couple who'd spotted them through the window earlier.

"Oh crap," Skye whispered. "Get down."

They both ducked, hoping to be hidden by the nearest lounge chair, and watched the couple's feet as they passed by the pool area.

"Do you think those freaks are still at it?" the woman said.

"God, I hope so," the man answered.

"You're sick. What kind of people have sex with the curtains open?"

Nico bit his lip to keep from laughing, and beside him he could sense Skye trembling with suppressed laughter. The footsteps got farther and farther away, until the sound of a door opening and closing assured them it was safe for them to come out of hiding.

"Okay, now I'm embarrassed," Skye whispered.

Nico sat up and dusted off his forearms. "Now? If you weren't embarrassed a few hours ago, I'd say you're a hard-core exhibitionist."

Skye scooted back onto their blanket. "I think every writer secretly is. It's that desire to put yourself out there in the world that leads people to write in the first place."

"But you're putting your books out there—not yourself."

"It's a very personal thing, writing a book. No matter how far removed what I'm writing is from my real life, it's still a part of me. Sending my work out always feels kind of like running down the street naked."

"And you know what streaking feels like?"

She swatted him. "I can imagine, anyway."

"I'd like to see that," Nico said, then realized his mistake. "But that's not an invitation to go running naked down the street right now."

Skye rolled her eyes. "I wouldn't do it for real."

She finished her taco, and after her last bite, a piece of lettuce still clung to her lip. Nico reached out and wiped it away.

"You just had a little bit of lettuce…"

"This is why I shouldn't be allowed to eat in front of other humans. It's bound to lead to embarrassment."

"Don't be embarrassed. I like women who wear their dinner well."

She smiled, her face radiant even in the darkness, and they sat watching each other, a comfortable silence filling the air between them.

Nico wanted to trust her, but maybe everything she did was part of a bigger plan. Maybe even the lettuce on her lip had been part of her effort to make herself seem human and vulnerable, disarmingly cute.

It was possible Martin had known Nico's weakness for Skye all along. Hell, anything was possible.

What did he expect? A written guarantee of Skye's trustworthiness? That was just plain stupid…as was his worry over whether he could trust Skye.

Being betrayed so thoroughly left him feeling overly suspicious, he knew. He was bound to think anything and everything was part of some elaborate deception.

He just needed to get past the insecurity and live his life. The worst that could happen was that he'd be deceived again.

At least that thought didn't make him sick to his stomach the way it would have a few weeks ago. Martin's con had caught him at a time when he was feeling a little weak for having given up his career. His lack of direction, his lack of a plan for the future, had left him vulnerable, and being so thoroughly scammed had made him feel like the world's biggest fool.

It hadn't helped that Martin had pulled the wool over his eyes at the same time that he'd had the woman Nico wanted. His envy of Martin's relationship with Skye had only compounded his feelings of insecurity.

It didn't do him much good to fume about it all

though. This kind of thing called for action, not self-pity, and somehow, some way, Nico would get even with Martin once and for all.

SKYE KNEW their luck was going to take a turn for the better when she woke Sunday morning to find a copy of the *L.A. Times,* a big box of doughnuts—fresh ones even—and a steaming cup of coffee sitting on the nightstand. She yawned and stretched, then spotted Nico sitting in the chair next to the broken table. He was sipping coffee as he thumbed through a magazine, and he looked divine in the morning light.

"You've already gotten up and gone out?"

He cocked an eyebrow. "Either that or some benevolent thieves broke in and left breakfast for us."

"Smart-ass."

She pushed herself up in bed before realizing she was naked. Then she remembered the way they'd nearly broken the bed, too, last night. And that had been after taking a forbidden dip in the pool following dinner.

She couldn't remember the last time she'd felt so insatiable for a guy. Maybe never.

Nico's gaze dropped for a moment to her bare chest, but Skye ignored him and grabbed the doughnut box. "Mmm, glazed. My favorite."

"I think we're too late to catch that bus to Death Valley," he said.

She shrugged. "That sounds like a bad omen, anyway—a bus to Death Valley. Could anything good come of a trip with that name?"

"Probably not. I can think of better things to do anyway." He tried to set the magazine aside, then remembered the table was broken and tossed it on the dresser.

She watched him move to the bed, then stretch out next to her as her body warmed to the memories of the night before. "What do you have in mind?"

"You, me, the bed. I figure we probably can't get into any major trouble if we don't leave the room."

"I like the way you think."

She opened the lid on her coffee, inhaled the delicious scent and took a sip.

Sometime between falling into bed with Nico the first time and the tenth or twelfth or fifteenth time, Skye realized all of a sudden that she'd started trusting him. She no longer feared he was trying to con her or take advantage of her or anything else.

Which meant she was probably being an idiot.

"You look like you're deep in thought," he said.

"I was just thinking that I probably shouldn't trust you."

"Because I'm such a shady lowlife?" His tone and expression were sarcastic, but Skye knew she'd offended him more than he was letting on.

"Because I have a long history of trusting the wrong guy."

"Can't you believe that sooner or later you'll accidentally trust the right guy?"

Skye laughed. "It would definitely have to be by accident."

"Maybe your doing-the-opposite strategy is working, crazy and improbable as it sounds."

She shrugged, a confused jumble of emotions welling up inside her. "I don't know. I mean, I keep getting confused about what I'm supposed to be doing or feeling."

"How so?"

"Like, if I do the opposite of what my instincts tell

me to do—for instance, by going on this trip with you—and then that puts me in a situation like this…"

"Feeling like you should trust me, you mean."

"Yes. When do I stop doing the opposite?"

"You're probably overthinking this, you know."

Skye tugged the sheet up over her chest and took another drink of coffee. It was strong and black, and while she usually drank it with milk—that is, before she'd officially sworn off caffeinated beverages—today she was in love with the taste of it straight. And she was feeling more alert by the minute.

"How can I *not* overthink it? I clearly haven't been doing enough thinking about all my prior encounters with men."

"Every guy you date isn't going to be a scumbag or a con artist. You have to first accept that you are fully capable of having a successful relationship with a man."

"Thanks, Dr. Phil. I'll try to keep that in mind," she said, then smiled into her cup as she took another sip.

He swatted her on the thigh. "I'm serious. Your lack of self-confidence is probably what got you to this point in the first place."

Skye plucked a doughnut out of the box and took a big bite as she tried to wrap her brain around the idea. Was she really lacking in self-confidence? She'd never thought of herself that way, but…

"Oh my God, that's it! I'm one of those annoying women who thinks they can't do anything right."

"I wouldn't call you annoying, but you don't seem to have a very accurate sense of your own abilities."

She glanced over at him and smiled. "Maybe we've just found your next career—pop psychology guru."

"Could you stop being a smart-ass for five minutes?"

She pretended to give the idea some thought. "I think two minutes sans smart mouth is my max."

"I think you need a good hard spanking."

"Mmm, now you're talking."

"I'll let you finish your breakfast first."

Skye took another bite of her doughnut, but she was losing her appetite. Was the answer to her relationship problems really as simple as getting some confidence? Or was Nico simply trying to make her believe she was doing the right thing in going on this ridiculous trip?

Maybe what she really needed was just to remain guarded. If she stayed cautious about trusting him, then she'd be less likely to get hurt again. Regardless of how much she wanted to believe he was someone worthy of her trust, she just had to keep in mind her track record to know the right course of action.

She could have great sex without trust though.

And probably it was better that way. It meant she could get what she needed without the accompanying hurt feelings that had gone with all her previous relationships.

It meant that for the rest of the day—maybe for the rest of the trip—she could be one amazingly satisfied woman.

13

It ALMOST seemed like a miracle when they pulled out of Tito's lot Monday with the Ferrari's windshield replaced. And an even bigger miracle when, an hour and a half later, they caught the glimmering view of the Las Vegas strip skyline from the freeway.

Nico was pretty sure he'd never been so relieved to see a bunch of neon lights.

"Wow, we made it," Skye said. "Now what?"

"Now we go to the lingerie shop where that red bra was sold, and from there, we follow the trail and see where it leads us."

He'd called ahead and gotten the address for the shop, which was located inside the Serengeti Hotel and Casino, in its main shopping promenade. Nico found their destination and parked in the short-term lot outside the casino. Then they got out and walked the distance to the side entrance.

Inside, they were already in the shopping promenade, and judging by the lit map near the entrance, they just needed to make a right and walk past five stores to find Lolita's Creations.

The casino's indoor mall was filled with upscale shops of the sort that charged a couple thousand dollars for a shirt or a pair of pants. No matter how much money he might have earned racing, he'd never understand the need to pay too much for things that weren't actually any more durable or valuable than their hundred-dollar counterparts.

Skye spotted Lolita's Creations first and tugged him toward the entrance, undistracted by the display in the front window. He took an appreciative look at the long-limbed mannequin clad in an ornate pink bustier and matching thong panties, then let himself be led into the store.

Nico glanced around the place, spying items left and right that would have looked amazing on Skye. He made a mental note to do some shopping before they left.

Skye bypassed the racks of bras, panties and nightgowns and headed straight for the saleswoman standing at the counter in the middle of the store.

"Excuse me," she said, digging the bra out of the shopping bag she'd used to carry it in. "Do you know anything about this bra?"

The woman, tall, blond and probably around the age of forty, wore a small gold name tag announcing that her name was Candace and she was the store manager. She took the bra and looked at it front and back. "It's from our store, I can tell you that."

"Do you custom-make lingerie?"

The woman nodded. "It's a premium service, and we don't actually make the lingerie here. We special-order it from a custom atelier for our clients who are willing to pay the price."

"Any chance you'd remember the person who bought this bra?" Nico asked.

Candace frowned, staring at the bra. "What's this about, anyway?"

"We're looking for someone, and the only clue we have right now is this," he said.

"Are you two detectives or something?"

"No, we're just playing detective for the sake of finding a wanted criminal," Skye said.

More information than Nico wanted to divulge, in the remote case that this woman knew Martin herself, but they'd failed to talk earlier in enough detail about what they should and shouldn't say.

Luckily, the woman seemed to open up when she heard she could be helping a good cause. "Do you know around when it was purchased? I keep a record of all special orders, so it's really just a matter of checking them."

"That's wonderful," Skye said. "We'd truly appreciate any help you can give us with this, but we're not sure when the bra might have been purchased."

"Definitely longer than a month ago, but that's all we know," Nico added.

Candace stared at him for a few moments. "You look familiar—are you a celebrity or something?"

Nico shook his head. "Not really."

"He's being modest," Skye said, looping her arm around his and patting his bicep. "He's Nico Valletti, the racecar driver."

The store manager's face lit up. "I knew it! My ex-husband used to watch Indy racing nonstop. I couldn't stand it, but I watched it with him sometimes just to catch a glimpse of you," she said with a smile and a wink.

It wasn't the first time Nico had heard that story. He smiled, hoping whatever he did to endear himself to Candace would get them one step closer to Martin. "I'm flattered."

"Any chance I could get your autograph?"

"It would be my pleasure," he said, turning on his most blatant charm.

She opened a drawer and withdrew a pen and note-pad, then handed it to him. Nico signed and handed it back, not at all bothered, he realized, that people didn't recognize him as often as they once had and didn't ask for his autograph nearly as often as they used to.

He'd loved racing and enjoyed talking to fans, but he'd never enjoyed being a celebrity the way some people did. He'd just as soon have his privacy, and maybe, if nothing else, the accident had given that back to him.

"Okay, so this wasn't bought in the past month," the woman said, typing on the computer keyboard that sat on the counter. She read something on the monitor, then typed some more. "I handle most of the special orders," she said. "And I do think I recall a woman buying this bra—maybe around six months ago, if memory serves."

"It seems like a pretty unusual order," Skye said, eyeing the detailed beadwork as she held the bra up to the light.

"You'd think, but you'd be surprised how many double-D cups and above we get in here on a regular basis. We're one of the only custom lingerie shops in the city, and Las Vegas has more than its share of sur-gically enhanced women." Candace typed some more, then took a step back and smiled at them.

"You found it?" Nico asked.

Skye peered at the screen. "Ruby Jewel, 4914 Calle Caliente, Las Vegas."

Nico read over her shoulder. A phone number was listed along with the name and address. And below that, the specifics of her order. "That's the name of the woman who bought the bra?"

"Her stage name, more like," Skye said.

"She's a regular customer here, so I'd really appreciate it if you could keep quiet on how you found her."

"Of course. We won't let her know we've been here," Nico said.

"Do you know anything about her besides her bra size?" Skye asked.

Candace appeared to be doing her best to recall. "I believe she's a showgirl over at one of the older casinos on Fremont Street. Maybe the Starlite."

"Any chance she's ever come shopping with a man?"

"No, I think I'd remember that. She's always been alone when I've helped her."

Skye jotted down the name, address and phone number from the computer screen. "We really appreciate your help," she said to Candace as she folded up the piece of paper and put it in the pocket of her mini-skirt.

"Anything else you can recall about this woman?" Nico asked.

"She's real friendly, not married as far as I know, loves to shop. Takes care of herself, probably tans more than she should, has long, dark-red hair and green eyes."

"Thanks," Nico said. "You never know what information might come in handy."

He wandered over to a rack of lacey black bras and matching panties, then picked out what he guessed were Skye's sizes in each.

"What are you doing?" she asked.

"Shopping for you."

"I don't really need any underwear right now."

He cast a sidelong glance at her, but said nothing.

"Really, I don't."

"I'm allowed to buy stuff without your permission, you know."

"I've got a little baby doll that would just look amazing on you," Candace said, hurrying across the store.

She returned with a sheer, hot-pink sequined thing in hand, and Nico nodded. "We'll take one of those."

"No, we won't," Skye said.

"And one of these, too," he said, grabbing a long black satin nightgown that laced up the sides.

Skye gave him a warning look, which he smiled at and ignored.

She leaned in close to him. "I can't afford all this stuff," she whispered. "And I don't want you buying lingerie for me."

"Why not?"

"I just don't!"

"Too big a commitment for you?" he asked.

"It reminds me of Martin, okay?"

Nico felt a rush of some inappropriate emotion. Possessiveness? Disgust that Martin had ever been lucky enough to spend a second with Skye? He didn't stop to analyze.

"I'm not Martin, and I don't have anything in common with him besides the fact that I'm crazy about you, okay?" he blurted.

He'd never tried to articulate out loud the way he felt about Skye. But *crazy about her* was a pretty damn good description. And it sounded a lot more PC than *obsessed*.

Still, she didn't exactly look as if she was ready to hear the news. She blinked at him, shock softening her features.

"You are?" she finally whispered, apparently not wanting Candace to overhear.

"Of course I am."

"Wow."

He'd hoped for something more than *wow,* but he figured he'd better be happy to get anything besides a slap in the face. Skye didn't seem to be the most enlightened woman when it came to her own romantic relationships or the emotions that went along with them.

Her wacko doing-the-opposite strategy was a case in point, but he couldn't really complain when it seemed to be working to his advantage.

Of course, there was the whole other problem of what he'd do with her if she did fall for him the way he seemed to be falling for her. He'd spent his whole life racing from one woman to another, and while lately he'd gotten tired of it, he wasn't sure if he'd ever want to be entangled in a long-term commitment.

His father's death and the way his family had later fallen apart, his own checkered love life, his abruptly terminated career—Nico had learned the hard way that life never worked out the way anyone planned.

"Why don't we discuss this later. For now, just relax and let me do some shopping."

Fifteen minutes and six hundred dollars later, they left the store and walked through the casino to the car. Okay, so maybe Nico couldn't justify two-thousand-dollar pants, but he could think of more than a few reasons to buy overpriced panties for Skye, not the least of which was getting her into them—and out of them—later.

In the car, he powered up the air-conditioning to ward off the desert heat, then got out the Las Vegas map to look up the street where Ruby Jewel lived. For the first time since Saturday, he had a sense that they were well on their way to finding Martin. They just had to follow the trail of the red bra.

SKYE WAS TRYING hard not to freak out.

Nico? Crazy about her?

He'd declared so himself, but it hardly seemed that it could be true. And then there was the lingerie shopping spree. What the hell had that been about? Okay, so maybe he was just trying to endear himself to Candace even more, or thank her for her help, or whatever, but…

But Skye couldn't get past the fact that he really seemed to be into her. And she really seemed to be into him.

Which absolutely, positively meant they were doomed.

She didn't want to fall into another doomed relationship. But it was a catch-22. The only way to have a relationship was to fall in love, and the only thing that was assured to happen when Skye fell in love was disaster.

Catch-22. No way around it.

Damn it, damn it, damn it.

She felt sick to her stomach, knowing that whatever good thing she might have found with Nico was doomed. Unless, somehow, some way, the Theory of Opposites could save them.

Was it possible? She hardly dared to hope.

Realistically, she knew the thing she was supposed to be focusing on now was tracking down this Ruby Jewel woman and finding out what she knew about Martin and his whereabouts.

"So, if this Ruby chick is home," Skye said to Nico, "what do we do?"

He struggled to straighten out the map while the

air-conditioning vents were blasting cold air. "We have to consider the possibility that she's still in contact with him—maybe romantically involved still—and act accordingly."

"So we can't just go barging up to her door and act like we're his enemies."

"Exactly. We need a cover story."

"Maybe we're friends of his, and he told us she'd know where to find him when we got to town?" Skye offered.

"That might work."

"What if she's not involved with him at all though? Then won't she know we're lying?"

"We could say the last time we heard from him was a month or two ago."

"But we don't know when she was last in contact with him," Skye said.

"It's possible she might know who we are—I mean, if she was in on Martin's con in L.A...."

"Then she could have known that he was living on your property and dating me."

"Exactly."

"Damn it."

"And if she's aware of his criminal activities, she's going to get pretty suspicious about anyone knocking on her door and asking about Martin."

"I don't think there's any way to avoid that. We'll just have to hope she's not that well-informed. If he was lying to everyone else, why wouldn't he be lying to her, too?"

"Maybe we need some kind of disguise," Nico said.

"Or just one of us. If I approach her alone, it might not feel so threatening to her. Maybe if he's left her, too, I could even play the scorned female card so we'd have something in common."

"Or I could talk to her alone. I've been told women find me attractive," he said in a deadpan tone that made Skye smile.

"Don't let it go to your head," she said. "What kind of disguise would you wear, anyway? A Fabio wig?"

"So now you're a comedian? You'd better stick to the writing thing."

"I'm serious. Would you dress in drag? What?"

"Okay, maybe you should go talk to her in disguise."

"Exactly. I'm not as noticeable as you—especially not to a woman."

Nico studied the map index, then flipped the map over and traced his fingers across until he came to the grid square containing Calle Caliente. Skye stared at the map until she'd semi-memorized the route to Ruby Jewel's house.

"I wonder where the nearest wig shop is," she said.

"This is Vegas—there must be one nearby."

Skye dialed information on her cell phone, and they quickly had the address of a wig shop only a few blocks from the casino. Soon they were standing inside the arctic air of the Wig Emporium. Skye shivered as she looked around the place, trying to picture herself looking convincing as a honey blonde, or maybe a raven-haired vixen.

Ha. She could do vixen about as well as Nico could do drag queen. She just didn't have it in her to be a temptress or a sexpot. She was too busy obsessing over how her ass looked from every possible angle to relax and seduce anyone.

Nico hadn't seemed to mind. Nor did he claim to see the inherent problems with her ass. She supposed she should have been grateful to him for that, but instead, it made her wonder what he was hiding.

No guy could be as seemingly perfect as Nico without having some huge, atrocious hidden flaw—could he?

"How about this one?" Nico asked, holding what looked like the remains of a raccoon in his hand.

They'd managed to beg off the attention of the sales clerk, winning themselves a little privacy to wig-shop in peace. If such a thing were possible.

"How am I going to hide all my hair under one of these without looking like I've got a watermelon-sized head?"

"Maybe you need a hat, too."

"A wig and a hat—that won't look obvious at all." Skye frowned into the mirror as she tried on a long blond wig. "Yikes, I look like Paris Hilton on crack."

"You've got that two-toned hair look going on. It looks kind of like you meant for your hair to be dark underneath," Nico said, not sounding totally convinced of his own words.

"Or kind of like I've got a blond wig sitting on top of my brown hair."

"Maybe if you try a larger wig, it'll hide your hair better," Nico said, scanning the mannequin heads for an alternative.

"How about that curly light brown one," Skye said, pointing to the display wall.

Nico got it down and brought it over, then Skye spent a few minutes tucking her hair under it. When she finished, she peered at herself in the mirror.

"It looks good," Nico said.

"Not as fake as the last one, definitely." In fact, Skye could hardly recognize herself. Gone was her long, limp do, and in its place was hair with enough body and curl for three women and a small poodle. The light-honey color even looked pretty natural on her.

"I don't think you'll need a hat with that one."

"I don't think we'd find a hat big enough to fit on my head with this one." She looked at herself one more time. "Okay, let's buy the wig and get out of here."

In no time, they were on the road again, heading out toward the western suburbs, where businesses gave way to new tracts of housing. By the time they made it to Ruby Jewel's street, they'd concocted a cover story for Skye, and she was mentally prepared for the conversation.

She'd pretend to be a woman who'd met Martin in L.A. and who he'd told he had a business venture he'd wanted to get her involved in. She'd claim Martin had given her Ruby's name as a contact in Las Vegas, right before he'd disappeared. Then she'd say she was in Vegas for the week anyway and thought she'd look up Ruby to see if anything had been heard from Martin since his disappearance. She'd act worried—like a concerned friend.

Maybe the cover story wouldn't work at all, but it was the best they could come up with.

Nico circled the block so they could check out the house, then parked around the corner, out of sight.

"Be careful, okay?" he said. "If she threatens you, just yell for help. I'll be right outside the house listening at the window."

"Don't you think the neighbors might get suspicious and call the police on you?"

"I saw an oleander bush I should be able to hide behind. It's right under the front window on the left side of the house, so stay near that area if you can."

Skye's stomach rolled over and played dead. Suddenly, it struck her how scary this whole charade was, and she wasn't at all sure she could handle it.

"Maybe this is the stupidest idea we've had yet. Maybe we should just turn what we know about Ruby Jewel over to the police and let them handle it."

Nico cast a sidelong glance at her. "If you're scared, we can leave now. Don't do this unless you're sure you can handle it."

Skye took a deep breath and exhaled. "Okay, the worst that could happen is, she'll kill me, chop me up into little pieces and shove me into the garbage disposal."

"Maybe you should just stay outside on the doorstep. How about that?"

"What do I say if she invites me in?"

"Say you just have a few questions and don't have time to come inside."

"What if there's some important clue about Martin's whereabouts inside her house?"

"You won't be able to find it if you're dead."

"This is freaking me out."

"Then I'll go talk to her."

"No—forget it. I'm being a wuss. I'll go, but I'll stay outside."

"Okay, and I'll be around the side of the house, in case there's any trouble. You're going to be fine, I promise."

Right. Just fine. She was about to go talk to the woman who'd likely been having an affair with her ex-boyfriend while she'd still been madly in love with him.

The thought didn't even set that badly with her, actually.

Maybe she really would be fine.

14

SKYE GOT OUT OF the car before she could lose her nerve again and hurried along the sidewalk toward Ruby's house. Behind her, she could hear Nico getting out of the car, but when she looked over her shoulder, he was going in the other direction, around behind the houses, where she had to assume he planned to sneak up from the back.

She walked up the sidewalk of Ruby's house and rang the doorbell. There was a lamp on inside the front window, barely visible, but at least a sign of life. She heard footsteps, and then the door opened.

Standing before her was a woman she'd never seen before. Long red hair, a vaguely pretty face, a large chest encased in a turquoise sports bra that looked as if it might give way at any moment, and a tiny waist and hips in black yoga pants.

"May I help you?" the woman asked.

"Hi. Are you Ruby Jewel?"

Skye felt herself relax by a degree. This didn't look like a woman who'd drag her inside and kill her. Ruby looked like a woman who'd just had her workout interrupted by a knock at the door.

"Yes," the woman said, looking vaguely perplexed. "That's me."

"I'm sorry to bother you. My name is…" Crap. She'd

forgotten to think of a fake name. "Fiona Van Derringer." Crap, crap, crap. Fiona was going to kill her. "And a friend of mine, Martin Landry, gave me your name as a point of contact to get in touch with him."

Ruby's expression transformed from cautious to pissed off in a nanosecond. "*Martin?* If you see that rat bastard, you can tell him I'll cut his dick off if he ever shows his face around me again."

Skye blinked. "Oh. I guess you two didn't part ways on good terms."

"Damn right we didn't. Slimy son of a bitch took off with all my credit cards."

"I don't mean to pry, but is there any chance you visited him while he was living in Los Angeles?" Skye asked, relieved that she and Nico weren't alone in their victim status, but more confused now.

Ruby nodded. "How did you know that?"

"It was just a guess."

"I met Martin a few years ago when he was living here in Vegas. I was married at the time, but he kind of had a thing for me. We went our separate ways on friendly terms, so I looked him up in L.A. when I was there a couple months ago, and we got even friendlier, if you know what I mean."

Skye wanted to puke, but instead she nodded with a sympathetic smile. "Martin's got a way with women."

A scummy, lying, cheating way.

"I was a little surprised when he showed up here a few weeks ago, saying he'd moved back to Vegas. But we hit it off, and then all of a sudden, I woke up last weekend and he was gone—along with my credit cards and two hundred bucks from my wallet."

"Wow. You never heard from him after that?"

"No. I called the cops, but there wasn't much they could do since I didn't actually see him take the money. I cancelled my credit cards, but he'd already charged quite a bit on them."

"I'm sorry to hear that."

"Yeah, me, too. Why are you looking for him, anyway?"

Skye made a face. "To be honest, he cleaned out my savings account, and I want my money back."

"I wish I could help, but I don't have a clue where he might be."

"Do you know if he has any friends here who might know where to find him?"

"Hon, if I knew that, I'd track him down myself."

"Do you have an address where he was staying?"

Ruby frowned. "You know, there is a guy over at the Monte Carlo, a blackjack dealer he hung out with sometimes. You might try talking to him."

"What's his name?"

"Clive Gaither. He's a big guy, olive skin, lots of hair on his body and none on his head. He's probably the closest thing Martin had to a friend. I'm sure the police have already talked to him, but it never hurts to try yourself."

Well, it might hurt. If Clive Gaither turned out to be a murderous thug or something. But spurred on by her minor success with Ruby Jewel, Skye felt optimistic.

"Thank you so much," she said. "I really appreciate your help. Could I leave you with my cell phone number in case you think of anything else that might be useful?"

"Sure," Ruby said. "Let me grab a pen."

She disappeared for a moment, then came back with

pen and paper in hand and gave them to Skye, who wrote down her fake name and her real cell phone number.

After they said goodbye, Skye walked back down the street and around the corner to Nico's car, then waited the few extra seconds it took him to arrive and unlock it. Inside again, she exhaled and relaxed against the passenger-seat headrest.

"You okay?" Nico asked.

"Fine. I'd make a terrible PI though. I can't handle the stress."

"Sounded to me like you handled it perfectly."

"Thanks, but I was terrified. I guess I probably shouldn't admit, though, that I felt better when she said Martin had ripped her off, too."

"You think she was telling the truth?"

"It hadn't occurred to me that she might be lying." Skye closed her eyes in an effort to keep her head from spinning. "I don't know. She seemed genuine."

"We don't have any choice but to hope she is, and check out this Clive guy at the Monte Carlo. Do you feel up to going over there now?"

"We might as well. I can't help but think that if Martin's best friend is a blackjack dealer, then he must have had some kind of scam going on with the casino, you know?"

Nico started the car and headed back out of the sub-division. "I think I've got a better idea than going straight to Martin's friend. I did some promotional work at that casino a few years ago, and I know the manager. Maybe he could give us some insight on this guy before we talk to him."

Hope swelled in Skye's chest again. She opened her eyes and smiled. Maybe they really weren't wasting time on a wild goose chase. "It's pretty handy having you around, you know?"

"You're just now realizing my usefulness?"

Skye decided not to answer that one. She'd found all sorts of fun uses for Nico, but saying out loud how much she liked having him around would mean giving voice to her biggest fear—that she'd fallen hard for him. Which meant that any second now, their explosive, crazy-hot chemistry was going to blow up in their faces.

"NICO VALLETTI, it's great to see you!" the casino manager said as he welcomed Skye and Nico into his office. "What brings you back to the Monte Carlo? Business or pleasure?"

"A little of both," Nico said, taking a seat with Skye on the cushioned sofa near the door.

"It's the Las Vegas way," the manager, whose name was Tom Meredith, said as he sat in a plush green chair opposite them. "What can I do for you?"

"I'm hoping you can provide me with some information on one of your employees, a man named Clive Gaither."

"What kind of information?"

"We're actually looking for a man who's a wanted con artist, and he's rumored to be a friend of your employee. We're thinking that either Clive is in with him to pull a con in the casino, or else the man we're looking for is pulling a con on your employee."

"Do you have a photo of this con artist? I can have security review their videos, see if they come up with any activity involving your guy."

"You can look him up on the FBI's Web site. The

photo there is the only one available—his most recent alias is Martin Landry."

The manager spun around and made a note of the name on a note pad on his desk.

"Any chance you could print the FBI photo for us, so we can use it to show around the hotel?" Nico asked.

"No problem. Just give me a minute here."

They waited while the manager brought up the Web site and printed the picture.

"Thank you," Nico said when he took the paper bearing Martin's image.

"I've got to tell you, it would be pretty damn hard to pull a scam inside my casino. There's plenty of easier targets he could choose than here."

"I've considered that. Really, I just need to know whether if I approach Clive to question him is he going to get suspicious and tip off Martin that we're on his tail."

"All my employees have spotless records. Anything less and they don't get hired. That's really all I can tell you about him."

"I appreciate your help," Nico said.

"Where are you staying? I'll call you when I hear back from security about your guy."

"We're at Caesar's Palace, checked in under my name."

"I'll give you a call in a few hours. Does that work for you?"

"I'm not sure if we'll be there, but leave a message if we're not. Thank you."

"While you're here," Tom said, "please, stay and enjoy yourself on me." He withdrew a plastic card from his pocket and handed it over.

Nico took the comp card, figuring if nothing else, it

would give him and Skye a chance to scope out Clive Gaither before they talked to him. "Thanks again."

He and Skye went down to the casino and wandered around, hand in hand. She'd kept her wig on, and Nico occasionally found himself wondering who the stranger was standing beside him. He much preferred her natural hair, but it was kind of a turn-on to see her with this entirely new look, too. And he fully intended to take advantage of the situation if he got the chance.

"You look pretty hot in that wig," he said as they stood watching a game of roulette.

"It's itchy," she said, trying to scratch her head without dislodging her hair.

"What do you say we skip the gambling and go to the hotel right now?"

"I'd say you're thinking with the wrong head. Let's at least see if Martin's friend is working this shift."

"Okay, okay."

He led her to the blackjack tables, and as they wandered, it didn't take long to spot the large man with the hairy arms and shining bald head.

"Wow," Skye whispered. "I wouldn't want to get on his bad side."

"I could take him," Nico said, half joking. At six feet even, Nico was tall for a racecar driver, and he worked out enough to stay ripped, but he was far from burly. He'd always been on the lean side, but going to a rough high school had taught him how to fight like a guy twice his size.

"You're such a guy," she said, elbowing him in the ribs.

"That's usually not something women complain about."

"I'm not complaining. I'm just sayin'. You need to keep your caveman urges in check if you want to be a smooth operator like me."

"I think all this investigating is going to your head. You've gone from scared shitless to smooth operator in the space of an hour?"

Skye smiled mysteriously and swiped the comp card out of his hand. She was such a mix of irresistible and infuriating qualities, he was powerless against her charms. One minute she was obsessing over her doing-the-opposite theory, and the next she was flirting shamelessly.

She was his hottest fantasy come to life.

"Why don't you just step back and watch a true smooth operator in action?" she said, and Nico tried not to laugh.

"Go for it, high roller."

He followed her around the casino and watched her lose five hundred dollars in about ten minutes, alternating his attention between her lousy gambling skills and Clive's presence at the blackjack table.

When she caught him staring at Martin's friend, she said, "I guess you're not as impressed by me as I thought you'd be."

"Sorry, babe. How about you continue your high-roller act at Clive's table?"

She shrugged. "I don't know how to play blackjack, but I'll try."

He explained the rules to her as they went to Clive's table. There they waited for the current game to end, but just as she took a seat, the dealer shook his head. "Sorry, ma'am, this was my last game. I'm going on break, but you're welcome to try another table."

"Actually, we were hoping to talk to you for a few moments, if you have the time."

Clive glanced at his watch. "I've got a minute. What's up?"

"Do you know a man named Martin Landry?" Skye asked.

Nico added, "That name is one of his aliases, and we're not sure what name he might be going by now, but we were told he's a friend of yours."

Clive looked from Nico to Skye and back again. "What's this about?"

"The man we're looking for is a wanted con artist, and we're hoping you might know something that could help us find him."

"Are you kidding me? I work in a casino. I'd be crazy to hang out with a con artist."

Nico withdrew the police photo from his pocket. "This is a photo of him. Have you seen this man before?"

Clive glanced at the picture, and his expression went hard. "That piece of shit? Yeah, I know him, but if he shows his face around here again, I'm gonna kick his ass straight out of Vegas."

It was hard not to notice a pattern forming. Martin left angry victims wherever he went.

"Did he try to rip you off?" Nico asked.

"He tried to get me involved in some scheme he'd cooked up to rip off Monte Carlo customers. I told him no way—you try to pull the slightest crooked crap here and your ass is busted. We got security cameras everywhere."

"Do you think he might have gone to another casino?"

"You got me, man. All's I know is, I didn't want any part of it."

"Any chance you know how to get in touch with him?"

Clive ran his hand over his bare head, giving the

matter some thought. "I didn't know much about him. We met at the bar here, and we got together for drinks or going out to clubs for a short while."

"You didn't have a phone number for him?"

"There was one time he had me meet him in the lobby of the Mirage. I just assumed that's where he was staying, but I never asked."

Skye handed him a piece of paper she'd just written her phone number on. "This is my cell. Would you call us if you think of anything that might help us find him?"

"Sure, I guess. He rip you off or something?"

"Something like that," she said, her face betraying the truth.

They thanked Clive for his time and left the casino.

"What do you say we change hotels tomorrow and set up shop at the Mirage?" Nico said as they got in the car to leave.

"Sure," Skye said. "It's not much of a lead, but it's all we have for now."

15

SKYE FELT like a new and improved woman. She'd showered in their luxury suite, then lounged around the room making love and playing with Nico in the hot tub until dinner time.

Plus she'd eaten lobster and baby asparagus for dinner. In one night, they'd managed to make up for all the fast-food meals and sleazy motel rooms.

They'd wandered the strip after dinner, found a nightclub where they'd danced until her muscles ached, and now they were wandering through a hotel she couldn't remember the name of, trying to find their way back to the entrance. Instead, they seemed to be in an endless maze of shops and restaurants.

Nico glanced down at her high heels. "Want to take a break from the walking?"

"Sure," Skye said and tugged him over to the faux rocks that lined the faux creek meandering through the center of the hotel.

"I've had fun tonight," he said. "And you look amazing."

Skye had worn her little black going-out-clubbing dress with its plunging neckline and uneven hem. She'd bought it envisioning a night something like this one, but she'd never imagined Nico would be a part of that night.

In his tailored Italian black pants and his black silk T-shirt, he was the one who looked amazing.

"I'm barely keeping up with you," she said.

"How did you decide you wanted to be a writer?" he asked out of the blue, then watched her as she thought about her answer.

"I guess I've always known. I mean, I was always making up stories as a kid, and the first time I ever put one on paper, it felt incredible. Like I'd discovered what I was meant to do."

"You're lucky you know what you're here for."

"Yeah, I just need to convince an editor."

"I've always admired creative people. I don't know how you just make up a story out of nothing."

"I guess it's kind of a defense mechanism. Whenever life starts to suck, I can just get lost in my own head, you know?"

"I bet you were one of those little kids who always got caught daydreaming in class."

Skye winced at the thought of her school years. Being creative and neurotic hadn't exactly endeared her to her classmates. "Yep, that was me. And I had plenty to escape from in those days. I definitely wasn't one of the popular kids."

"Get out of here. A girl as pretty as you?"

"I was dorky and awkward as a kid. Never pretty."

"I don't believe you. I'm going to need to see pictures to believe it."

Skye tried to imagine taking Nico home to her parents' house and getting out the family photo albums. She was surprised to realize she could totally imagine it. No doubt her parents would love Nico.

Scary thought.

"I may have destroyed all the evidence of those years, but if there's any left, I'll be sure to show it to you. You were probably one of the popular kids, right?"

He shrugged. "I went to a pretty rough school. It was more survival of the fittest than a matter of popularity—at least in my mind."

"And you survived. Thrived, even."

"Something like that."

She tried to picture Nico as a kid but couldn't. He was so much larger than life, so right here and now, all she could summon was the image of him as she knew him now.

It was late—almost one in the morning—and around them the crowd of tourists had thinned out.

"We should probably find our way out of here and get some rest, don't you think?" she said, not altogether hopeful that they'd find Martin at the Mirage, but not ready to give up yet.

"Are you okay with walking again?"

"My feet thank you for the break—I'm definitely ready."

"You sure? I can give you a piggyback ride."

"I don't think this dress was designed for piggyback rides—at least not public ones."

He took her hand and they wandered some more, but instead of finding the exit, they found their way to a door that led out onto a large balcony that overlooked the strip.

"Wow," Skye said as they stepped up to the stone balcony wall and looked out at the glittering lights. "It's like an amusement park on steroids."

"We have a view just like this from the balcony in our room—why don't we go find it?" Nico said, his hand sliding down her waist to her backside.

Skye warmed to his touch, her body coming alive the same way it had when they'd been dancing together an hour ago. Nico was a great dancer, a little better than her, but he'd made her relax enough that she hadn't embarrassed herself.

"I'm afraid we might be trapped in this place forever at the rate we're going."

"I can't think of anyone I'd rather be trapped with," he said pulling her against him now.

His hips pressed against her backside, he slid his hands around her waist and down her thighs, then up under her dress.

The night air was still warm, but the exposure of her bare flesh to it sent gooseflesh skittering over her.

"What are you doing?" she whispered, not really worried about the answer.

Whatever he was doing with his hands exploring her, she was game.

"I'm getting impatient. I don't want to spend all night trying to figure out how to get out of this damn hotel when I could be having you instead."

"Maybe we should ask for directions," she said as his hands found her breasts and squeezed her nipples.

"I'm a guy. I don't ask for directions."

He kissed her neck and her ear, and his erection pressed into her backside, driving her crazy with wanting him.

"We're just going to do it right here then?"

"No one's around," he whispered. "And you've already proven yourself an exhibitionist."

Skye looked out at the strip and sighed as he slid one hand down her belly and dipped into her panties. His fingers found her clit and started massaging. She gasped. She was already slick and ready for him, already burning to feel him inside her.

It was true. She liked doing what they shouldn't have been doing right here, where they might get caught. Probably there were security cameras recording their every move, and she didn't care. It only made her hotter.

His fingers dipped inside her, and she gasped. Down below a couple of cars honked their horns, and someone yelled. From somewhere far away, she could hear bass-thumping music coming from what was probably a car stereo.

"I want you inside me now," she said as she arched her back and rubbed herself against him.

"Damn it," he said. "I just realized all my condoms are back in the hotel room."

"What are we waiting for—let's go," she said, trying to wriggle out of his grasp.

But he held her still, his fingers inside her. He rubbed her clit again, and she melted back against him.

"There's no reason we can't have a little appetizer right here, before the main course," he said.

Skye couldn't think of any reason to argue that. Well, really, with her body so coiled with desire, she couldn't do much thinking at all.

He turned her around and pushed her back against the stone wall, then pushed her dress down to expose her breasts. Then he dipped his head and took one breast into his mouth as he plunged his fingers deeper inside her, deeper and deeper still, until she could feel her inner walls begin to quake at the edge of orgasm.

"You're already there, aren't you?" he asked as he trailed his tongue up her chest to her neck.

She tangled her fingers into his hair and held on, unable to answer with more than a sigh.

He dropped to his knees then, surprising her. He pushed up her dress, pulled down her panties, pushed her leg up to rest on his shoulder. Then he plunged his tongue into her.

Skye gripped the wall and arched back, aware of little but the sensation of his tongue inside her, his breath against her, his hands holding her tight to the place she most wanted to be.

A moment later she could resist no longer, and her body gave in to the delicious quaking that began deep at her core and traveled outward. She bucked against his mouth, crying out with the release, unsure if the bursts of light she saw were from the city below or her own orgasm.

When she stilled, he placed kisses on her thigh, her belly, and up to her chest and neck. Finally, her mouth. She drank him in, kissing him with all the hunger he'd created in her. She couldn't imagine wanting a man more than she wanted him. So wildly, so insatiably, so completely.

"You," she whispered when they broke the kiss. "You make me crazy."

"In a good way or a bad way?"

"Definitely a good way, unless we get arrested one of these times."

"Let's get the hell out of here," he whispered, then placed a kiss on her forehead.

She smiled. "Okay."

He could have suggested they do a swan dive off the balcony at that moment, and she probably would have been game. That was when she knew, without a doubt, she was back to letting her stupid, worthless instincts do the decision-making again.

And somehow she had to stop it.

16

SKYE HAD pretty much given up hope of finding Martin at the Mirage. He wasn't checked into the hotel under any of his known aliases, and they'd spent all of Tuesday morning searching the hotel and its surroundings with no luck. Not that they'd come to expect any sort of luck, but with Martin's trail turning cold now that they were finally in Vegas, she wasn't sure what was left for them to do except give up and go home. They couldn't keep divining information from lingerie and questioning strangers forever.

As she rode the elevator down to the lobby, she reviewed the facts in her head one more time and came up with nothing. The manager at the Monte Carlo had claimed there'd been no suspicious footage of Martin, though he had shown up there to gamble on various occasions. They'd gotten no calls from the other leads they'd spoken with, and no one at the Mirage recognized Martin's photo.

If she'd had to sum up their situation now, she'd say they were screwed.

The elevator reached the lobby, and Skye stepped out and glanced around the casino. For the first time since arriving there, she felt a little naked, as if she should have been wearing her poodle wig and some big sunglasses or something.

She'd left Nico in the room, claiming she needed to find a drug store where she could buy some cosmetics because she'd run out of a few essentials, but really she just wanted to go outside where she could get a good signal on her cell phone and talk to Fiona with some privacy.

Maybe Fiona would know what to do about the fact that she was falling for Nico and couldn't seem to summon the will to defy her instincts any longer. She wanted what she wanted, and that was that.

But she knew what happened when she felt this way. Relationships came crashing down, CD collections disappeared, bank accounts emptied. Hearts got broken.

Surely there were big danger signs all around that she was too stupid to interpret. But maybe if she could describe the past few days to Fiona, her best friend could spot the warning signals she'd missed.

She weaved through aisles of slot machines, skirted a cocktail waitress and rounded the turning display of a Mercedes that large signs promised would be the prize for one lucky winner of something-or-other. Only a little bit farther, and she'd be at the side entrance.

Suddenly, panic seized her. She felt as if she were being watched, as if danger was near. She couldn't say why.

Glancing around, she hurried into the clearing. Her heart raced as she weaved through the maze of people entering and exiting the large glass doors. On the left was a gift shop, and she nearly screamed when she spotted a man who looked exactly like Martin turning from the counter where he'd just paid for something.

His hair was different—shorter and darker—but she had no doubt it was him.

In what was possibly her worst stroke of luck yet, he looked up and their gazes met. In the instant before she could react, she saw confusion, then comprehension cross his face. She pretended not to see him and turned toward the door, but from the corner of her eye she caught the movement of him coming toward her. A glance over her shoulder sent a jolt of cold fear through her. He was jogging now, casually as if he'd just spotted a friend and was trying to catch up.

Skye's mind raced for a plan. If she tried to get away, there'd be no chance of getting her money back. But if she was smart, she could convince him she was really in Vegas because she wanted him back. And then what? She had no idea. She'd have to figure that out later.

She passed a shop window display and stopped, feigning interest in it.

"Skye?" She heard Martin say from behind her.

She turned, wearing her best shocked and semi-outraged expression. "Martin!"

"Didn't you just see me standing there in the gift shop?"

"I thought you looked familiar, but it didn't register. I'm not used to seeing you with such short hair."

"What the hell are you doing here?"

Her eyebrows shot up. "I could ask you the same thing."

His expression went blank for a moment as he studied her, probably looking for signs of her real motives. "I needed to get out of town fast. I got into a little trouble."

"And you needed to borrow all the money in my savings account to do it?"

He glanced left and right. "I owe you an explanation about that, but let's not do it here. Why don't we go talk someplace a little more private?"

Skye's stomach flip-flopped again. This was exactly what Nico had warned her not to do. But, all her instincts were screaming not to do it, too, and thus far, doing the opposite had netted some success. She had to be brave and keep it up.

She and Nico had planned to corner Martin and call in hotel security if they found him, then turn him over to the police. Nico had argued that it was the safest plan—that maybe in police custody he'd spill the truth about where her money was. But now—now was her chance to find out on her own where her money was.

"I saw a little restaurant back that way," she said, motioning toward the casino.

"Why don't we go back to my room? I could be in a lot of trouble if anyone overhears what I have to tell you."

Don't do it, her instincts screamed. But she couldn't ask him back to her room, where Nico's belongings were scattered everywhere, and this was the big chance she'd been searching for.

She'd been with Martin for over a year, and he'd never once done anything physically threatening to her. He might have been the world's biggest liar, but she seriously doubted he was aggressive.

"I guess that's okay," she said. "But we're just going there to talk, and then I'm leaving. You got it?"

"Of course," he said.

Maybe this would work out to her benefit. If she could convince Martin she still trusted him, and that she still had romantic feelings for him, then she might gain his trust long enough to figure out where he'd put the money.

He slipped his hand around her waist and led her toward the elevators. That one intimate contact left her cold. A few months ago, she would have fallen naturally into his affection, would have seen it as a sign that he was The One.

She was such a freaking idiot.

"What's with the brown hair?" she asked as they walked, playing dumb. He was naturally blond.

"I just needed a new look," he said, and when they stepped onto the elevator alone, he added, "I've got to be honest with you, Skye. I'm in some trouble. I had to change my hair to keep from being spotted."

Her eyes widened in mock disbelief. "What kind of trouble?"

"Haven't the police been in contact with you?"

She sighed. "They told me your name wasn't really Martin, that you're some kind of con artist or something, but I wasn't sure what to believe."

He gave her an affectionate smile that made her want to puke. "That's my girl. You know you can trust me, right? Even if I couldn't tell you the whole truth back in L.A.?"

Skye bit her lip and pretended to give the matter some thought. "I don't know. I mean, I want to trust you, but you're going to have to give me a good explanation for why you ran off, and why the hell you took all my money."

The elevator stopped on the fourteenth floor, and they exited. Martin led her down a long corridor, and Skye felt a delirious sense of fear building inside her. It took all her willpower not to bolt.

"I'm so sorry I had to do that. I'll pay it all back, plus interest, okay? And when all is said and done, I'll have enough cash for that luxury cruise to Tahiti you've always dreamed of."

What a load of crap.

They stopped at room 1422, and Skye tried to make an emergency escape plan—elevators down the hall, to the right, signs for the staircase to the right—as Martin unlocked the door and stepped aside for Skye to enter. The room was dark, its curtains closed against the bright sun outside, so she switched on a light and walked to the middle of the room, where she stood looking around casually, pretending she wasn't trying to spot a place where her money might be hidden—like maybe in a big treasure chest with chains wrapped around it or something.

Okay, seriously, he probably had the money tucked away in a bank account somewhere, but one never knew about the financial habits of a con artist.

"I've missed you so much," Martin said as he walked toward her.

Skye crossed her arms over her chest. No way was she letting him touch her, and if he thought she would, he had a hard kick in the balls coming to him.

He caught her body language and held up his hands in defeat. "I know, I know. You're waiting for an explanation."

"That would be nice."

"Why don't you sit," he said, motioning to the bed.

Instead, Skye went to a nearby chair and sat, crossed her legs and waited for him to start talking. Martin sat on the edge of the bed across from her and leaned forward, his elbows on his knees. He looked tired, and maybe a tiny bit nervous.

"I had this business deal that went bad, and I was really worried about you getting hurt if I stuck around you any longer. I didn't realize the people I was dealing with were serious scum until it was too late, and they started trying to extort money from me, claiming if I didn't pay them every month, they'd keep the money I'd already invested and kill me."

Skye tried her best to look shocked. She wouldn't have been surprised now if he were involved in criminal deals, but the old Skye—the one Martin had known—would never have guessed it.

"Oh my gosh, Martin. That's awful."

God help her if she was as terrible an actress as she imagined.

"I know," he said. "It was scary as hell. I didn't know what to do, and I was afraid if I told you what was going on, you wouldn't understand."

"And you thought I *would* understand if you took off with all my money?"

"I'm sorry, sweetie. I was desperate. I didn't know what else to do, and I just needed to get away before they started looking for loved ones of mine they could threaten, too."

"So what exactly did you do?"

"I was flat broke from losing the money they'd already extorted from me, so I got your bank information, withdrew the money, and went into hiding."

"Don't you think they might come looking for you here?"

"I just wanted to stay here long enough to win some money at the blackjack tables, and then I was going to find a new place to settle down—but not before I gave you the chance to come with me."

"You thought I'd want to go into hiding with you? After you emptied my bank account?"

He sighed, a pained expression crossing his face. "I wasn't thinking straight. I was scared as hell, and

I just prayed that once you heard the truth, you'd forgive me."

She pretended to give the matter some thought. It wasn't hard to look betrayed and confused, because she pretty much was, but the challenge came in giving a convincing performance of her faux transition from betrayed to forgiving. Skye channeled her inner Meryl Streep and hoped for the best.

"I don't know. This all sounds so crazy. I mean, I come here for a weekend getaway, and I end up finding you instead. I guess I just need some time to let all this sink in."

"Of course you do." He reached out and took her hand in his, then held it the same way he used to whenever they were close.

Skye realized that she'd been right about how empty she felt with regard to Martin. All the love really was gone, and so was all the hate. There was just a blank place where he used to fill her with those emotions.

Then Nico popped into her head. She'd been afraid her leftover feelings for Martin were making things too complicated with Nico, but if there were no leftover feelings, then what?

Skye slid her hand out of Martin's and wiped off her damp palm on her leg.

"When did you plan on getting in touch with me?"

"When I felt like it was safe. I needed some time— for those thugs to forget about me, and for the police to stop looking for me."

"Oh."

"I love you, Skye. Just as much now as I did then—even more, actually. I've missed you so much. I never imagined we'd run into each other this way, but seeing you brought it all back. Can you please forgive me?"

Her gaze met his, and she nodded slowly. "Maybe I shouldn't," she said. "But I do."

He smiled. "I knew you'd come through for me, baby. We're just too good together."

"We are. I don't know how I'd ever find another guy like you."

Another lying, cheating, thieving scumbag like you.

The room was surprisingly sterile. No signs that anyone had stayed there, no traces of Martin anywhere. Probably he was always prepared to vacate at a moment's notice.

Martin stood up and offered his hand to her. Skye let him pull her up to a standing position in front of him, but if he tried to kiss her...

No ifs about it. He was heading straight for her mouth. She coughed. "Excuse me," she said stupidly, then coughed again.

"Are you coming down with something?"

"I just had a tickle in my throat."

"You don't want to kiss me, do you?"

"I have to admit, I might need some time. I mean, for the past month, you've got to understand I was harboring some pretty nasty feelings for you. I can't just make them all go away with one quick conversation."

"I know, baby. I know." He pulled her closer and hugged her, and the scent of his cologne that used to give her warm fuzzies made her want to barf now. "I'm so sorry," he murmured into her hair.

Skye couldn't deny he was a damn good actor.

"Listen," he said. "I've got a lunch meeting in about a half hour that I can't miss."

"Don't mind me," she said. "I could just wait here for you, or meet you later."

"Give me just a minute to clean myself up, and I'll take the elevator downstairs with you. We can meet up again later tonight. How's that?" he said, heading to the bathroom.

Nico would never go for her meeting Martin for dinner. He'd be too worried about her safety to approve of her meeting with Martin alone in the hope of getting any more information out of him.

Skye tried to imagine what excuse she'd use to explain to Nico that she'd be out for the evening, but nothing came to her. She'd have to think of something later.

For now, she had to do what little she could while Martin was in the bathroom.

She sprang up from her seat, her gaze locked on the bathroom doorway, went to the edge of the bed and lifted the mattress as far as she could. Nothing there. She dropped to her knees and peered under it, all the while listening for movement from the other side of the room. Martin was whistling as he did his thing in the bathroom, giving her a gauge for his location.

The space underneath the bed was empty, too, so she stood and eased open the drawer of the nightstand, which revealed only a Bible and a brochure for the hotel. But Martin would never be dumb enough to hide something important in such an obvious place as a drawer.

She put her hand inside the drawer and ran it along the top, to see if anything was taped there. No luck, so she closed the drawer, then ran her hand along the underside of the nightstand. Her fingers brushed over something flat and covered in plastic. Catching her fingernails under the edge of it, she gave the plastic thing a good tug, and it detached from the dresser.

When she pulled it out and saw that she was holding a zip-lock bag full of cash, her heart leapt in her chest. Dizzy with her unexpected success, she jammed the plastic bag under the waistbands of her skirt and panties, then stood up to see if there were any other hiding places close by she could search.

But the whistling stopped, and Skye spun around to see Martin staring at her.

"What the hell are you doing?"

"I, um, I was looking for any signs that you've been cheating on me," Skye stammered, trying to summon some jealous feelings.

Martin's expression went from hard to curious. "Did you find anything?"

"No condoms in the nightstand, no women's underwear under the bed." She shrugged. "Those were the only places I had a chance to look."

Her insides had turned cold. She was playing a game that could get her killed, she realized for the first time. If Martin was deceptive enough to convince her he was an entirely different person, then he was also a good enough actor to hide any dangerous impulses that might lurk inside him.

But now he was coming closer, and he had that look in his eyes—the one he always got when he had amorous intentions.

"Baby, there's no other woman I want besides you."

Yeah, her and Ruby Jewel, and probably her old neighbor who'd introduced him to Skye, and who knew how many other women.

He reached out and ran his fingertips along her cheek

and into her hair. With his other hand, he pulled her to him. Then he gazed into her eyes.

Skye willed herself to relax, act like this was sort of what she wanted.

"How can I be sure of that?" she asked.

"I'm trusting you to be here right now with me, aren't I? I could have bolted when I saw you downstairs. For all I know, you'll call the police and have me arrested first chance you get."

"Why do you trust me so much then?"

"Because I love you, Skye. No matter what happens, you'll always be the one for me."

He dipped his head and kissed her then, and it took every ounce of her willpower not to push him away. He plunged his tongue into her mouth as if they'd never been apart, while rubbing his hands along her spine and over her backside.

She tried to respond as if she weren't averse to the whole thing, but after a few agonizing moments, he sensed her coldness and backed off. Thank God. Any closer and he would have felt the bulge of the plastic bag under her skirt.

"What's the matter?"

"It's going to take time, Martin. I can't just snap my fingers and suddenly trust you after what happened. I want to, but I guess I just need to see some proof that you're telling me the truth."

"The proof is all right here. Can't you feel how much I want you?" he said, grinding his erection into her hip, coming dangerously close to the bag.

Oh sure, like any straight guy with the right hardware wouldn't have the exact same reaction to a willing female.

"I feel the way you want *something*."

"I'm not twenty-one anymore, babe. I don't get an instant hard-on for every woman I kiss."

Skye sighed. This whole conversation was going in the wrong direction, but before she could come up with a suitable way to tell him to back off, Martin said, "I've got maybe fifteen minutes. Come on, baby, let me remind you why we're so good together."

He slid his hands under her shirt and was going for her bra. She tried to wriggle away, but he held on tighter when he felt her pull back.

"I can't right now," she blurted. "I stopped taking birth control when you left."

"I've got condoms in my wallet."

Slime ball.

"You're so broken up about us being apart that you had to make sure you've got extra condoms on hand?"

"Don't be like that, Skye," he said, dipping his head to kiss her neck. "I've had them there for I don't know how long out of habit—that's all."

Skye wriggled out of his grasp. "That's a load of crap and you know it," she said, crossing her arms over her chest, glaring at him.

"Okay, I deserve that." Martin glanced at his watch. "Let's talk about this later, all right? Over a nice, romantic dinner."

His mysterious meeting—probably with the nearest bus out of town. Skye had to think quick about how she'd keep Martin from running. But if his reaction to her upon spotting her downstairs was any proof, he wouldn't run. Maybe Nico had been right all along—maybe Martin really had loved her.

And she wasn't sure whether to be happy about that or even more freaked out.

"Why don't we meet downstairs in the lobby," she said. "Is seven good for you?"

Skye nodded and headed for the door, her insides so keyed up with nervous energy, she felt as if she were vibrating.

"I'll see you later then," she said, forcing a smile.

He stopped her at the door and gave her one more kiss, this one not so possessive. Skye made a mental note to brush her teeth the first chance she got, gargle with mouthwash and give herself a good scrubbing to remove Martin's slimy residue.

_17_

SKYE RAN the short distance to the elevator, then banged on the button until it arrived and boarded it as if wild dogs were chasing her. It was empty, thank goodness, so she pressed the button for the concierge level, inserted her special security card, and then pulled the bag of money out from beneath her skirt.

There was a hundred-dollar bill on top. And at first glance it looked as though the bag contained about ten grand.

Ten thousand freaking dollars. In one crazy instinct-defying act, she'd recovered her savings. She bit her lip to keep from squealing.

She ran back to the suite, opened the door and saw Nico put down the phone and turn toward her. He stared at her like she'd reappeared from the dead.

"Where the hell have you been? I was worried sick."

"I wasn't gone that long."

"I thought you were just going right downstairs and coming back. I was afraid you'd run into—"

"I did! And we have to hurry," she said. "I found Martin—or rather he found me. He's staying on the fourteenth floor in room 1422, and if we go downstairs now, we can probably catch him."

"We need to call hotel security," he said. "Let them catch him."

"He doesn't look anything like the photo we gave them—he's got short brown hair now—so we need to be downstairs to ID him. He's leaving his room any minute now."

"They can stake out the elevators or something." Nico went to the phone, called hotel security and explained the situation.

When he hung up, he turned to Skye again.

"So what should we do?" she asked.

"They said we should stay put, but I don't want to see him get away. There's only one bay of elevators, so let's get downstairs now, and we can be there when he comes down."

They hurried back to the elevator, and Skye pulled out the bag again. "Look at this. I think there's ten grand in here!"

"Where the hell did you get that?"

"Long story. Martin spotted me in the lobby, so I couldn't really get away from him without being obvious. And surprise, surprise, he didn't bolt. He thinks we can pick up right where we left off or something."

"What did he say to you?"

Skye gave him a rundown of the whole encounter, and Nico's expression grew darker the more she talked.

"Are you insane? You went to his room alone, and you never once thought to call me, or call the police, or get the hell out of there?"

He looked her up and down, as if the answers to his questions might be found on her person.

"I got this money, didn't I? And I got out safely. There's no point in second-guessing now."

The elevator stopped, and two middle-aged women boarded, halting their conversation for the time being.

Two floors later, they were in the lobby, and they stepped off the elevators and looked around.

"Now what?" Nico said.

"I don't see security anywhere," Skye said as she turned around, surveying their surroundings.

No sooner had the words left her mouth than the farthest elevator opened, and Martin stepped out.

Skye grasped Nico's arm. "Hide," she whispered. "Quick!"

But it was too late. No sooner had the words left her mouth than Martin spotted them. He turned back to the elevator, just as the doors closed, and finding that route cut off, he bolted to the left, toward the hotel promenade.

Skye suddenly wished she'd packed at least one practical pair of shoes. Strappy jewel-embellished heels were far from ideal for running, but she took off with Nico after Martin as best she could, dodging tourists and slowly falling behind as Nico pulled ahead.

Soon she had only a view of his back as he chased Martin, and all she could do was jog behind, cursing the entire way. She saw Martin bolt to the right, with Nico following behind, and then they both dodged a velvet rope barrier and went into some kind of tourist attraction called the Deep Space Experience.

The attendant yelled after them, then picked up the phone and dialed security. Skye stopped at the counter. "Tell them the man in the white shirt is a wanted criminal," she yelled at the attendant while the woman was still on the phone.

Skye turned to go into the dark corridor that led to

the exhibit or ride or whatever it was, but the attendant hung up the phone and said, "I'm sorry, ma'am, but you have to buy a ticket to go in."

Skye fumbled for her wallet, pulled out some bills, and threw them across the counter. She got her change and her hand stamp, then ran in the direction where Nico and Martin had disappeared. Inside, she made her way through the maze of black walls and twinkling white lights, until some kind of emergency buzzer started going off, and she heard male voices calling out from what sounded like the center of the exhibit.

"Nico!" she called out but got no answer.

She heard the sound of footsteps running toward her, and then Martin rounded the corner and stopped in his tracks when he saw her. He seemed to consider his options for a split second, and then he bolted toward her and grabbed her by the hair.

"Make one bad move and I'll break your neck," he said as he locked his arm around her neck and held tight. "You help me get out of here, and I'll let you go—you hear?"

Skye nodded, his hold on her neck too tight and her terror too great for her to form words.

"You stupid little whore, I can't believe you led Valletti right to me. And the freaking cops! I thought we were for real, Skye. I'm disappointed in you."

She closed her eyes and tried to think as he backed her deeper into the exhibit. Tried to remember a self-defense lesson that might help, or something she could say, anything that might save her.

She'd just glimpsed a side of Martin she'd never seen—the scared, cornered Martin—and she didn't doubt that he was capable of violence now.

"Okay, everybody! Listen up!" he called out when they'd reached the center of the stage, where a display of stars and planets were showing on the screen.

"Anyone make a wrong move, and I'm going to break the girl's neck. You hear that, Valletti? I've got Skye, and as long as I get out of here, she won't get hurt. You got it?"

"Just calm down, man. No one needs to get hurt," a male voice called out.

Skye could barely see the seats in the audience, and only a couple of people were sitting there watching the show. She could see Nico now, standing near the back of the dark room, and to his right were three security guards, with guns drawn.

"Okay," Martin whispered in her ear. "I want you to tell them you want to leave with me. Tell them if they let us leave, you'll be okay."

She still couldn't talk. She could barely breathe, thanks to his hold on her neck.

Then she remembered the one bit of self-defense advice she'd learned in a class she'd taken with Fiona a few years ago. That toes were vulnerable and easily broken. One swift stomp could catch an attacker off guard and give her a chance to get away.

She summoned every ounce of her strength, drew up her foot and brought the pointy heel of her sandal down as hard as she could on Martin's foot.

"Screw you!" she said as he yelped in pain, and as his grip on her neck loosened, she twisted out of the hold and fell to her knees, then scrambled toward the nearest row of seats and dove behind them.

A gun shot rang out, and she heard Martin yelp again. When she peered over the top of the seat at him, she saw him sprawled across the raised platform as planets and stars glowed above him. A moment later, the security guards descended on him and had him in handcuffs. Skye marveled at the fact that he didn't seem to be seriously injured, and then she realized from the way Martin had beeen rubbing his chest—which wasn't bleeding—a few seconds ago, that the security guards must have been using rubber bullets. Nico grasped Skye and pulled her into his arms.

"Thank God you're safe," he said, holding her tightly.

She pressed her face into his neck and inhaled the scent that in the space of a few short, crazy days, she'd come to love. She felt his pulse against her cheek, and she relaxed into his arms. And for those few perfect moments, he was her entire universe.

NICO DIDN'T CARE about the money. Skye could have all that she'd found, unless the police needed it as evidence, in which case he'd make sure she got her savings back one way or another. He only cared that she was safe and Martin was in police custody. Everything else was insignificant.

Well, everything except his feelings for Skye.

They'd all come into focus for him today. This was no ordinary affair they were having. They'd crossed over from casual sex to something else. Something bigger. And he wanted to find out what it was.

For the horrifying moments that Skye had been in danger, Nico had understood with perfect clarity what she meant to him. She was the reason to find his new purpose in life.

Skye was shaking her head now as they walked to the main entrance of the casino, seemingly at a loss for words.

"Are you okay?"

"I just can't believe it's over. I mean, part of me never imagined we'd really find Martin, let alone see the police take him away in handcuffs."

They'd answered the police's questions, and now they were free to return to L.A. Mission complete. It was that simple.

But Nico didn't really want it to be over. Not having Martin to search for meant not having a reason to keep Skye in his life, unless she wanted to stay.

They walked along the hotel promenade without really having a destination.

"You want to grab something to eat?"

Skye shook her head. "I'm still pretty hyped up from that whole Martin encounter."

Up ahead, a lighted sign marked the entrance of the Deep Space Experience. Nico glanced down at Skye's hand, still stamped from when they'd chased Martin inside.

"I can't believe you got your hand stamped," Nico said.

"They wouldn't let me in without a stamp!" she said, then smiled. "That Deep Space thing was kind of wild, actually. Want to check it out for real?"

"Are you sure you're up for that?"

"I'm fine, really. I've already paid for the ride—it is a ride, right?"

"I'm not sure what it was." He'd been so busy trying to chase down Martin, he'd only gotten the vaguest impression of his surroundings. A huge movie screen full of outer-space stuff, eerie music, a platform full of seats that seemed to move.

"Okay," he said. "Why not? Let's check it out."

"Probably no one's even inside it now."

It was midafternoon, and the ride had been cleared out because of Martin.

"So we could be all alone in outer space? Sounds perfect right now."

Nico paid for his hand stamp, then they entered the black corridor with its twinkling overhead stars. This time, without Martin to follow, Nico paid attention to the details. The piped-in orchestral music—the sort that suggested alien beings might at any second appear and beam them onto the mother ship—lent an air of spooky mystery to the place, and the artificially cool air added to its otherworldliness.

They wandered the dark corridors that wove aimlessly through a maze of light displays, illusions and gusts of air until they reached the main room, where the movie screen and platform were.

Skye had been right. They were the only people there. They chose seats at the back of the platform, where it was darkest, and a few minutes later the show began.

Nico turned his attention to the planets and outer space stuff shooting past on the screen, but a moment later he felt Skye's hand on his thigh, and then she was sitting on his lap.

"You didn't think I really wanted to see this show, did you?"

He smiled. "I think you're breaking a bunch of safety rules right now. We're supposed to be wearing our seat belts."

"Call me reckless," she whispered right before she kissed him.

He could only take this as a good sign—and a sign that he should tell her how he felt while he still had a chance. They deserved a chance to see if there was anything more to their relationship than great chemistry.

But then the platform shifted back, and the chair with it. Skye balanced herself again, her hair tickling his face.

"I think this ride could be a lot more interesting," she said, "with you inside me."

Nico thought about protesting, but what the hell. She was unfastening his pants, and then pushing aside his briefs.

Her other hand slid down his belly to his cock, and her fingers teased the sensitive ridge of it until he couldn't stand it anymore. Just when he started worrying that he'd come in her hand, she stopped…lowered her lips to his…kissed him long and deep.

Nico moaned into her mouth as she began teasing his cock again. This time, her touch was lighter, and he loved that she could already read his body so well.

She had an instinctive sense of what he ached for, and she knew when to give it to him and when to hold it back. She could work him over like no woman he'd ever been with before, and maybe it was because she'd already starred in so many of his fantasies—long before he'd ever had a chance to have her live and in the flesh.

"Mmm," he moaned as she traced her fingers over the veins of his cock.

"You like that?" she whispered, just as the platform they were sitting on tilted again.

On the screen behind her, a glowing red planet came into view, and an asteroid shot past. A million glittering stars surrounded them.

"I like everything you do, you know. Want to know a secret?"

She smiled. "What?"

"I've wanted you since the first time I ever saw you going to visit Martin. I thought you were the most gorgeous thing I'd ever seen."

She looked at him as though he were crazy. Yet another thing he loved about her—that she was so beautiful and didn't even know it.

"That's insane."

"I'm serious. I used to watch you walking up my driveway and think Martin was a lucky bastard."

"I don't believe you."

"You wore a flowery dress one time, and the wind blew your skirt up around your head. You were wearing pink panties that day."

Her jaw dropped. "Oh my gosh, you saw that!"

He nodded.

"I wish you'd said something back then."

"And you would have left Martin for me?"

"Well, probably not. But who knows? I'd have been an idiot not to."

"I think you would have stood by him, because you're that kind of person. You wouldn't just up and leave your boyfriend because some other interesting offer came along."

"I guess that's the kind of attitude that gets me into serious relationships with con artists and other assorted scumbags."

"I'm not an assorted scumbag."

She started to say something, but stopped. Finally, with a smile playing on her lips, she said, "I never would have imagined we'd be like this together. So I'm glad, if nothing else, Martin gave us a chance to get to know each other."

"Me, too."

The ride tilted again, and Skye nearly slid off his lap. He caught her in his arms and pulled her closer. Her skirt slid up her hips, and he pushed her panties aside, then grazed his fingers over her clit.

She expelled a sigh and arched herself toward him, inviting him closer. He let his fingers slip between her lips, where she was hot and wet. Then he slid two fingers inside her tight pussy, caressing, in and out, up and down.

They kissed and stroked and licked in a wild frenzy, as if they were getting one last chance to experience each other.

The thought nearly stopped him cold, but then Skye's touch aroused him again, and he was lost in her. In all their desperation, he forgot to put on a condom before pushing himself inside her, and he was nearly over the edge from the intense sensation of her flesh against his when he realized their mistake.

He stopped pumping inside her. "I forgot protection," he said.

"Oh shit," she whispered. "I did, too. I've got something in my purse."

He tried to catch his breath as she dug around in her bag, and a moment later, she had the condom in hand and slid it on him. Without any more delay, he buried his cock inside her again and pounded harder and faster, determined that they reach their destination before the ride ended and they risked getting caught.

Skye matched his strokes, riding him, gasping as she held tightly to his shoulders, sending them hurtling into outer space and beyond.

And he understood that he was completely lost in her, unsure where she stopped and he began. This had to be as good as it got—he couldn't imagine ever topping this one perfect encounter. Couldn't imagine stopping…

Until he could feel her tightening around his cock, saw pleasure transform her features, and watched her shatter. Her orgasm brought his own, and as he spilled into her, stars shooting around them, he knew he'd just launched himself off into completely new territory, never explored before by his kind.

She melted against him as they caught their breath, and a moment later the ride stopped and the platform leveled out.

"Wow, great ride," she said.

Nico placed a kiss on her neck. "What do you say we stay here for the rest of the week together? Just hang out and have some fun."

"You mean here in Vegas? Or here on this outer-space ride?" She smiled, and he gave her a swat on the bottom.

"I meant here in Vegas. We'd better get out of this ride before we get arrested."

She stood and pulled her panties and skirt back into place, while Nico rearranged himself, disposed of the condom in a garbage can in the aisle and fastened his pants.

"Nico," she said, stopping him before he could head for the exit. "I don't think that's such a good idea."

"What?"

"Us, staying here. I've got to get home and start looking for a job, and—"

"Forget the job. That can wait a week, and you could take time to write while we're here. I promise I'll leave you alone—occasionally." He flashed a smile, but her expression turned more serious.

She seemed to be searching for the right words, and

as the lights brightened in the room, a final signal to them to vacate the Deep Space Experience, he could see that she looked as if she was about to say something she didn't want to say.

"I can't trust myself around you, Nico. When I'm with you, I just lose control, and I know, sooner or later, that's going to lead to disaster." Her gaze dropped to her feet, and when she looked back up at him her eyes had turned hard. "It always does."

"I'm not every other loser you've dated, Skye. I'm just a guy who wants to get to know you better."

She shook her head. "What we just did? That was my final test. I knew if I could come back in here with you—in a public place, where I had a guy threatening to kill me a few hours ago—and lose control again, then I'd have to end this right here and now."

"What?" He tried to wrap his brain around what she'd said, but it made no sense.

Maybe it was part of her dumb doing-the-opposite theory or something. Or maybe it was just the final result of his one-sided obsession. Could he really have believed staring out a window at some other guy's girl-friend could ultimately lead to a real relationship?

He'd gotten more than most guys ever did. He'd lived his wildest fantasy. Maybe he just needed to take that and be happy.

"I'm sorry, Nico," she said. "This was just sex. You've got to know that as well as I do. When we get together, we're like a couple of animals operating on instinct. I can't trust myself to make any intelligent de-cisions when I'm with you."

Nico opened his mouth to speak, but nothing came out.

"Thank you," she said. "For everything."

She leaned in close and placed a soft kiss on his lips. Then he watched her walk away.

SKYE STEPPED onto the bus and felt a sinking feeling all the way to her toenails. She avoided eye contact with the other passengers who'd already boarded and made her way to a row about halfway back, where both seats on the left were empty. She stowed her bag overhead, took the window seat, and buckled herself in.

When she was settled, she peered out at the bus station. How had she gotten to this point? How had even going against all her bad instincts still resulted in absolute disaster?

Tears welled up in her eyes when she thought of Nico, whom she hadn't wanted to hurt. She'd lied to him. It hadn't been just sex to her, but she knew herself too well to believe that their relationship had a chance in hell of success.

The part about losing control and not being able to trust herself had been the truth. The part about it only being sex and nothing more had been a big fat lie. She'd fallen for Nico, and now she'd have to get over him and move on. Maybe someday she'd find a guy she could trust herself with and whom she could go to public places with without fear of stripping off her clothes and making a spectacle.

Next to her, someone sat down, and she cursed silently. Of all the empty seats… She should have put her laptop down next to her. Skye glanced over and saw that her seat companion was a scruffy, leathery-looking woman of the sort who could have been thirty, forty or fifty. It was too difficult to guess without further staring, thanks to what looked like years of sun damage and hard living.

"Hey, hon. You mind if I smoke?"

"I think it's against the rules," Skye said, pointing to the no smoking sign at the front of the bus.

The woman waved a dismissive hand. "That's just for when the bus is moving."

"Oh." She thought about saying she was allergic to smoke, but before she could, the woman had lit up and was puffing away.

"You win anything?" the woman asked. "Oh, and by the way, I'm Betty."

"I'm Skye. Nice to meet you. I wasn't here to gamble. I came to…meet someone."

The truth seemed way too crazy to explain to a stranger.

"What the hell kinda name is Skye? Your parents hippies or something?"

"Um, yeah," Skye lied. It was easier than trying to explain the truth—that her parents were shallow enough to have been planning ahead for her career in entertainment. They figured they'd set her up for Hollywood stardom with her name alone.

She glanced out the window, hoping her lack of eye contact would dissuade the woman from asking any more questions. The last thing Skye felt like doing was chatting. She just wanted to wallow in her misery alone, without the distraction of strangers.

"I came to play the slots. Me and my best friend from Bullhead City meet out here every other month, and—"

Skye sighed, tuning out Betty's life story. She hated to be rude, but really, this was one time she just wished she could brood. She glanced at her watch. The bus wasn't departing for another ten minutes, wasn't scheduled to arrive in L.A. for another six hours.

She leaned back in her seat and prayed for sleep. Going home was going to be one long, miserable ride.

18

SKYE COLLAPSED on the bed and pulled the covers up over her head. If she lay really still, maybe Fiona would forget she was home and wouldn't ask any probing questions. Maybe she'd completely forget Skye had just returned from the road trip to hell.

Maybe she was hoping for too much.

Talking about what a mess she'd made of everything didn't sound even remotely appealing, but she heard footsteps coming toward her room, and she knew the inevitable was coming. A moment later, someone sat down on her bed.

"Was it really that bad?" Fiona asked.

Skye closed her eyes. Maybe she could pretend she was asleep. She tried to breathe slowly.

"Are you going to answer me or stay hidden under the covers all day? I know you're not sleeping."

"I'm staying under the covers. Pretend I'm not here."

Her sheets had a strange smell. She tried to remember the last time she'd washed them and realized it had been way too long. Eew.

Skye pushed the covers off her face and stared up at the ceiling.

"Pretending to be a corpse isn't going to work, either. I just saw your arms move."

"It was awful, Fi. Awful."

"Didn't you do the opposite?"

"I did—well, I tried. But it didn't work."

Fiona sighed. "Then I give up. There's just no explaining your bad luck with men. What happened?"

"What didn't happen might be a simpler question to answer. Let's see…I didn't get abducted by aliens. I wasn't kidnapped by terrorists. I didn't kill anyone… I think that covers it."

"Seriously."

"I'm not prepared to divulge details. It's all just too crappy to think about."

"Why didn't you call me every night like you said you would?"

"Because I didn't want to recount all the gory details when they were still so fresh in my mind."

"It couldn't have been that bad."

"Well, I guess since we caught Martin and found my money, I should call the trip a success. So how to explain why I feel like total and complete crap?"

"What if I bribe you with food and drink? Will you talk about it?"

"I'm not moving from this bed."

"I bought some new tea—orange ginseng. I'll make some for you."

"The last new tea you bought tasted like seaweed and flotsam."

"Um, I think that's what it was. It's the latest thing in health-food stores—the healing properties of flotsam."

Skye tried to keep looking morose, but she finally succumbed to the utter absurdity of it all and started giggling, which quickly turned into a deep belly laugh, which then led to tears that she could easily disguise as the laugh-until-you-cry kind.

"I'll pass on the tea," she finally said when she caught her breath.

She looked from the ceiling to Fiona and saw that her friend appeared far more worried than amused. "Are you really going to be okay? You're starting to freak me out."

"I guess that depends on your definition of 'okay.' Will I survive? Yes. Will I ever have a successful relationship with a guy? All signs point to no."

"Okay, how about if I find some peanut M&M's? Will that get you to talk?"

"What! You've had candy in the house and you've been holding out on me?" Skye sat bolt upright in bed, the prospect of chocolate energizing her.

"I bought it while you were gone. I couldn't resist." Fiona at least had the grace to look guilty. "I figured our healthy-eating pact was null and void if you were off eating restaurant food and stuff."

"Bring on the chocolate."

Fiona disappeared from the room and came back with a jumbo bag of peanut M&M's that looked to be about half empty. "All yours if you tell me what happened."

Skye reached out for the bag. "It looks like you've already eaten most of it."

"Actually, me and John." Fiona smiled, looking a little…something. She didn't get mushy very often, but she almost looked as though she was smitten.

"You two hit it off?"

"Something like that."

"You're going to see him again?"

"Something like that."

"Good for you. I'm glad one of us can claim romantic success in life."

Skye clutched the bag of M&M's. She stuck her face up to the opening and inhaled the chocolate scent. Then she grabbed a handful and shoved some into her mouth.

Fiona grimaced. "Hungry much?"

"Shut up," Skye said with her mouth full.

After a few more handfuls, she felt sufficiently fortified to recount the details of her trip, and by the time she'd finished telling the tale, Fiona was staring at her in complete disbelief.

"Wow. That's just…crazy."

"Now you know why I stopped calling. Who would have believed me?"

"You really had sex on a space ride?"

"Among other places."

"Wow."

"Please tell me I did the right thing in walking away from Nico. Please tell me I'm not a moron."

"You're not a moron. I mean, it sounds like you get even more crazy with him than you normally do."

"Exactly. It was just like the honeymoon phase of all my biggest disaster relationships—only amplified times ten."

"I'm sorry, sweetie. I know the right guy is out there for your somewhere."

Skye's stomach revolted at the thought, and she set the M&M's aside. "I'm finished with guys, dating and hot, sweaty sex for a while. I don't think I can be trusted around penises."

Fiona patted Skye's thigh. "Only certain penises. But don't worry, when you're ready, I'm going to find the right penis for you. Maybe it will have to be an electric one not attached to a guy, but I know there's one out there with your name on it."

Skye grabbed the nearest pillow and smacked her roommate in the head with it.

"That was so not funny."

"Sorry. Hmm. What are we going to do now?"

"Besides eat the rest of these M&M's? I was thinking of going out in search of more junk food, then curling up in bed and sulking for the next year or so."

"That's one option. But maybe you ought to do what I do—when I'm depressed I do my best creative work. Write your way through the pain."

"Writing and making collages are not the same creative processes. How can I write upbeat contemporary fantasies when my life is the exact opposite of that?"

"Should I go get my violin?" Fiona asked.

Skye gave her a look. "Ha. Ha."

"Because really, you're starring in your own docudrama here, babe."

"What a supportive friend you are."

Skye had a piece of peanut lodged between her teeth now, but the trek to the bathroom to retrieve some dental floss seemed like more effort than she could handle, so instead she popped another M&M into her mouth in the hope that the chewing might dislodge the peanut.

"I don't mean to sound snarky—well, actually, I do—but seriously, you need to lighten up a little. Put things in perspective."

"How so?"

"Your scumbag ex got what was coming to him, you got some closure, you're alive and safe, and you're now free of the racecar driver only last week you were calling Satan."

Skye sighed, realizing she was sounding more and more like a drama queen. She needed to get a grip.

"You're right. The thing with Nico, it was probably just meaningless sex."

"If that were true, you wouldn't be lying here like you'd just gotten a rejection letter from your dream agent. Oh, but speaking of agents, you got a letter with a return address from the Wainright Agency in the mail a few days ago."

"Perfect. A rejection letter from my dream agent. How appropriate."

"How do you know if you haven't even opened it?"

"If it's a rejection, it comes by mail. They always call if it's good news."

Fiona sighed. "I'm sorry I mentioned it. So, the Nico thing—I have to tell you, I think you're incapable of having meaningless sex, but just because it was meaningful doesn't mean it was worth pursuing. Okay? Just keep that in mind."

"I don't know. I mean, all my instincts were telling me to stay away from him, so I did the opposite, and then once I kept doing the opposite, I couldn't stop."

"Was he as good as he looks?"

"Better. Much, much better."

She could hear Fiona crunching on M&M's, then she said, "I'm going to need specifics."

"Underneath the perfect exterior, he's actually really sweet and interesting and not at all the stereotype of a celebrity. And he's got this sort of intensity that I just can't turn away from. It's hard to explain."

"You managed to walk away from Vegas without him. That's a sign that you're learning from past mistakes."

"Yeah, well. I didn't learn enough to keep myself

from falling for him, which unequivocally means there must be a scumbag somewhere in there, hidden beneath his perfect exterior."

"Oh, Skye…"

"I couldn't wait around to find out how he was going to screw me over—or how I was going to ruin everything. I knew I had to reverse my string of relationship mistakes and get out while I still could."

"But…well, sweetie, now that I think about it…"

"What?"

"I think I see the big hole in our do-the-opposite theory now. You see, if you follow the logic very far, you're never, ever going to have a long relationship with a guy, because every time you fall for someone you'd have to leave. Does that make an ounce of sense?"

"I thought of that, but seriously, I know it's only a matter of time until disaster strikes."

"You could say that about any relationship though. The true test of a good one is that it can weather the disasters, natural and otherwise."

"And the true test of a guy's interest is how he acts when you walk away. Nico didn't even flinch. Just let me walk, casual as he could be."

"Just because a guy doesn't beg or try to stop you doesn't mean he's uninterested. It means he's a guy, with all the limited ranges of emotion and lack of sensitivity that seems to plague that gender."

"I don't know. He almost looked relieved to see me go."

Fiona leaned forward and gave her a hug. "Next time I see him, I'm going to kick his ass for you, okay?"

"Okay."

"I've got a yoga class. Want to come along?"

Skye shook her head. "No thanks. I need to catch up on stuff around here.

After Fiona left the room to change into her yoga gear, Skye went into the living room and stared morosely at the stack of mail sitting on the coffee table that had arrived while she was gone. Several credit card bills glared at her—purchases of new jeans that probably would no longer fit on her fast-food-enhanced ass and a new designer bag that she wouldn't need since she had no spending cash to put in it and she would probably have to cut up all her credit cards in her newly unemployed state.

And then there was the dreaded agent's rejection letter. Not even the latest copy of *Cosmo* at the bottom of the stack could cheer her up now. She plucked the white envelope with the Wainwright Agency's name on it out of the stack and carried it straight to the recycling bin.

The last thing she needed right now was any kind of specific comments on why her writing sucked the big one or why she'd never get published in a million years. Without opening it, she tossed it into the recycling bin and heaved a sigh of relief. One more rejection letter down, probably a zillion more to come.

Maybe she should give up writing. Maybe Fiona had the right idea, finally taking a job with benefits and good pay so that she could move on with her life. She'd always have her art as a hobby, and maybe that would be enough for Skye, too.

She tried to imagine herself going back to work at the Club Sunset, and a heavy weight settled in her belly. She couldn't do it. She'd done a marketing internship in college—her last-ditch effort at having a backup plan before she set out into the real world and took publishing by storm. She could always get an entry-level marketing job, maybe even at the company where she'd interned. They'd offered her a job back then, but she'd turned it down, not wanting to sell her creative talents short.

Instead, she'd opted to find a mindless job that would leave her with all her mental energy to write at night and on weekends. Clearly, she'd made the wrong choice.

Skye went back to the living room and sat on the couch, grabbed the stack of mail and started opening her bills. First came her Visa card with the charge for the Coach bag. It had been a comfort purchase in the aftermath of Martin running off with her life savings. Sure, it was stupid to spend money when she had so little to spend, but she'd carefully worked out her budget and knew she could afford the splurge so long as she was really careful with her next few paychecks.

Except, now she only had one next paycheck coming, and it was going to have to go a hell of a lot further than she'd ever anticipated. She winced at the $427.92 total, which included the bag and a few other smaller purchases, plus a couple of dinners out. She'd always been careful never to put more on her credit cards than she could pay off at the end of the month, but now… Now she was pretty much screwed.

Too late to return the bag. She'd already used it. Maybe she could sell it on eBay though. Maybe she could sell everything on eBay.

Even if she'd recovered her savings from Martin, she wouldn't touch it now. That was her nest egg, the money she'd been setting aside for retirement and maybe buying a house someday.

She opened her MasterCard bill and gasped at the total—over eight hundred dollars. Most of it was for an unexpected car repair last month that had totally slipped her mind.

Biting her lip, she silently reminded herself not to freak out. She could handle this. She could find a way to pay the bills. Maybe she'd have to borrow money from her parents… Who would then give her a lecture on why she had to stop writing those teenager books and start writing something people would care about—like movie scripts.

Okay, so she wouldn't borrow money from her parents unless she got desperate. She'd sell all her belongings on eBay first, including Nico Valletti's underwear that had accidentally gotten stuck in her bag. Then maybe she'd cut off all her hair and sell it to Wigs 'R' Us or something.

She didn't realize until a fat teardrop splattered on her MasterCard statement that she was crying. She wiped off the bill on her jeans, then wiped her face on her sleeve.

This was ridiculous. She needed to be proactive. Go online to check her bank account and see exactly how bad the damage was. Then she'd really have a reason to cry. She went to her bedroom and took her laptop out of its bag, then sat on her bed while she waited for it to boot. The wireless system Martin had installed for her provided an Internet connection from wherever she wanted within the apartment, so once she'd logged on to her computer, she opened the Web browser and typed in the URL for her bank.

While she waited for the page to load, she opened her e-mail and downloaded the messages that had accumulated since she'd last been home. It hadn't even occurred to her to try to check e-mail while they were on the road, though surely at least their hotel in Vegas had had Internet access.

When she saw the message from Joanna Mays of the Wainwright Agency arrive in her inbox with the subject line *"The Cinderella Factor,"* Skye's heart sank. It was dated the previous Friday—the day before she'd left with Nico.

Perfect. She'd thrown away one rejection letter, only to find a rejection e-mail waiting for her, too. Did her dream agent hate her writing so much that she'd felt the need to tell her twice how much she sucked?

Skye highlighted the message, and her finger hovered over the delete key. But after a moment, curiosity won out and she couldn't resist opening the message.

Dear Ms. Ellison,
I've just finished reading your manuscript, *The Cinderella Factor*, and I'm happy to say I loved it. I would be thrilled to represent you and do my best to sell your book...

Skye blinked at the words, trying to make sense of them. Was this some kind of hoax? She looked at the sender's address—it appeared authentic—and then at the first paragraph again. She read it a second time, then a third, then a fourth. The words sank in a little more each time.

Then she moved on to the next paragraph, which explained that a contract was in the mail, asking her to look it over and sign it if she was interested in representation and agreed to the terms. There was also some mention of the agent having tried to call but getting no answer and no machine.

A contract. She'd thrown it in the recycling bin. Skye shot up from the bed, then ran toward the kitchen, not quite realizing that she was screaming until Fiona appeared wild-eyed in the hallway to stare at her.

"What's wrong?" she demanded.

Skye stopped, closed her mouth, shocked that such a primal screech could come out of her. "It's a contract!"

Fiona blinked. "Um. What are you talking about?"

"That rejection letter wasn't a rejection letter—it was a contract!" Skye said as she hurried into the kitchen and flung open the cabinet below the sink.

She pulled out the recycling bin and grabbed the white envelope, tore it open, and pulled out the folded papers. Her hands were shaking as she read the cover letter. Words like *loved your book, great characters, highly marketable* and *fun premise* jumped out at her as if they were images in a 3-D movie.

She started crying as she flipped over the page and saw the Wainwright Agency contract, just waiting for her to sign it.

"Skye! That's awesome," Fiona said as she hugged her.

The next few hours were a blur as Skye called Joanna Mays, asked all the questions she could think of about agency policies, how Joanna worked with clients, what kind of plan she had for submitting Skye's work, and confirmed that she really was as excited about working with Skye as Skye was about working with her.

By the time she had gotten off the phone, signed and mailed the contract, and come down from her high, she collapsed on the living-room couch in an exhausted heap. Just when she'd thought life would never finish kicking her while she was down, something miraculous had happened.

Somewhere between L.A. and Las Vegas, between losing the guy who was too good to be true and finding the guy who'd been nothing but a lie, Skye's luck had finally turned. And suddenly, impossibly, her dreams didn't seem so farfetched anymore.

SKYE WOKE to the vaguely achy feeling that came with drinking too many margaritas last night at the Mexican place where she, Fiona, John and a handful of other friends had gone to celebrate Skye's finding an agent. She stumbled from her bed to the bathroom, which was still a little steamy from Fiona having already showered and left for her pharmaceutical sales training.

She was trying to pry the lid off a bottle of aspirin when the phone rang. Not in the mood to talk to another human yet, she figured she'd let the answering machine pick up...until she remembered that the answering machine had conked out a month ago and had never been replaced—which was the reason Joanna Mays hadn't been able to reach her by phone.

She ran to the phone in the living room and grabbed it. "Hello?" she said, her voice gravelly from sleep.

"Is this Skye Ellison?"

The voice sounded formal, as if maybe it was a bill collector. "Um, yes," Skye said, wincing.

"I'm Lucy Ramirez, assistant to Robert Lavin, the CEO of Kid TV. Mr. Lavin has requested I schedule a meeting with you to discuss your idea for a new TV series, and I'd like to know when would be a good time for you to come in."

Skye felt that crazy urge to scream rising up in her chest again. She would not freak out this time. No. She'd be calm.

Media giant Robert Lavin was requesting a meeting with her.

Maybe this was a margarita-induced dream, in which case it wouldn't hurt to act cool and play along.

"My schedule is pretty much open," she said, making the understatement of the year.

"How about tomorrow at three o'clock? Would that work for you?"

"Sounds good," Skye said, impressed by the calm in her own voice. "Where are you located?"

She grabbed a pen and jotted down the address, then said goodbye and hung up the phone as casually as if she'd just made a dental appointment.

This had to be a dream. She walked back to the bathroom and stared into the mirror. Looking back at her was her usual puffy-faced, bed-headed, too-early-in-the-morning self. If it was a dream, would she really look this bad?

She pinched herself and it hurt like hell. She banged her toe good and hard on the bathroom cabinet, and it hurt even more.

Suddenly the suspicion that this was real sprang up in her foggy brain. Her aches and pains seemed to vanish as the idea settled in, and she realized that Nico had kept his promise. He'd said he would hook her up with the exec from Kid TV if she helped him find Martin.

And he'd done it. He'd really done it.

But she'd never taken that part of his offer seriously. She'd never once thought about what kind of television show she might pitch if she had the chance. She didn't even know anything about pitching TV shows.

She'd figure it out.

She went back to her bedroom, powered up her laptop, and opened her Web browser, then Googled How to Pitch a Television Series. In a matter of seconds, she had a ton of hits, and she clicked on the first one.

Then her idea came to her all at once, clear as day. *The Cinderella Factor* could be made into a series. It had all the important elements—a loveable teenage heroine, an endless array of plot possibilities, a wacky secondary cast of characters...

She could do it. She really could.

She'd get on the phone with her agent—her agent!—and talk over the possibilities.

She'd take all her formerly crappy luck and turn it upside down. Somehow, some way, she'd grab this opportunity and turn it into the answer to her dreams.

19

NICO STARED OUT at the crashing surf. The sky over the ocean had turned gray and foggy, reflecting his foul mood back to him. He walked along the beach that separated his house and his neighbors' houses from the ocean and tried to isolate the source of the unhinged feeling that had plagued him lately.

It was as if somehow, all of a sudden, he'd become detached from the world and at any second might just go hurtling off into outer space.

Sure, he had let some of his old friendships fall to the wayside after the wreck. It was as though his life was divided in two halves—before retirement, and after retirement. Even the word *retirement* bugged him. Made him feel as if he should have been wearing polyester pants hitched up high and socks with sandals. As if he should have been moving to Florida and playing golf. That kind of thing.

It was screwing with his self-image.

And then there were the girlfriends—or lack of them. He was beginning to realize he didn't want to live out his life as a guy women went to for sex and nothing more. Skye had taught him that.

He hadn't wanted to face the fact that his misery in the past week had come from not having Skye around, but there it was. He'd let himself fall for the wrong woman, and now he just needed to get over it and move on.

There was a hell of a lot of moving on to be done. He just wasn't quite sure how to get started.

"Hey, Valletti!" a male voice called from behind him.

He turned to see his next-door neighbor, Robert Lavin, jogging toward him. He was wearing a gray sweat suit with the hood up against the wind, and he appeared to have been jogging for a long while judging by his red face and heavy panting.

"How's it going?" Nico said when Robert stopped in front of him.

"Good if you don't count my being hopelessly out of shape. I just wanted to thank you for sending Skye Ellison my way."

"Oh yeah? No problem."

"I met with her earlier this week, and she's got a hot idea. I think we can work with it."

"Good for her. She's got loads of talent—she just needs a lucky break."

Okay, so Skye had never exactly let Nico read any of her writing, but he knew she was talented. Somehow, there was no doubt in his mind. He only needed to know her to know that whatever came out of her was worthwhile, adorable, funny and intelligent.

"She one of your girls or something?"

Nico winced. One of his girls? He'd turned into a caricature of a sleazy guy, complete with his own personal harem, apparently.

"No, we're friends. I mean, we might have had something going, but it didn't work out. No hard feelings," he lied.

There were definitely hard feelings. Hard, insurmountable, impossible-to-forget feelings. But Rob Lavin didn't need to know that.

"So what's keeping you busy, man?" Rob asked as he stretched his legs.

Nico shrugged. "Not much. I've been talking with a couple of investors about opening that fantasy racing camp, and everyone's interested in the idea of tying it to a charity for kids with debilitating injuries."

"Excellent. Keep me up to date on it. I can get you lots of media attention when you say the word."

"It's all about the right hype, isn't it?"

"Believe it. And when it's for a good cause, I'm more than happy to do my part."

Nico glanced up the beach at the Lavin mansion, with its stark contemporary lines and huge windows. On the balcony that spanned the length of the house stood Rob's wife, a white sweater wrapped around her shoulders. When she saw them looking in her direction, she waved.

"I think that's my signal for dinner," Rob said, his expression no longer exhausted. It was as if one glimpse of his wife had transformed him into a younger, more energetic man. "Hey, you want to join us?"

"No, that's okay, thanks. I don't want to impose."

"It's no imposition. The cook always makes extra."

Nico sighed. He would love a home-cooked meal, even if "home-cooked" meant prepared by the neighbor's chef.

"Well, if you're sure Karen won't mind—"

"Come on, she'll love to have the company."

Ten minutes later, Nico sat in the Lavins' cavernous dining room with its wall of windows overlooking the beach. He liked Karen Lavin, and he was glad for the chance to catch up with her and Rob.

But now, sitting at the dinner table with the two of them staring at him, he felt as if he'd accidentally wandered into an inquisition room.

On the plate in front of him sat an exotic looking salad with only a few ingredients he could actually identify. He stabbed a red leafy thing with his fork and took a bite, then was pleasantly surprised by the taste.

"Rob tells me you're still leading the swinging bachelor life," Karen said. "No promising women around yet?"

Oh hell—the dreaded when-are-you-going-to-settle-down? conversation. It was as though married people had joined a cult and would never be satisfied until they'd recruited the entire world to join up, too. They looked upon single guys like him—eligible and over thirty—as puzzling curiosities, meant to be examined and then matched up with the next available female as soon as possible.

"There was someone, but it didn't work out," he said, surprising himself.

He was usually a lot more vague in response to such questions. But being here in this house that felt so much more like a home than his own empty, too-large place did, his guard was down.

Karen raised her eyebrows with interest as she sipped her white wine.

"I'm intrigued. Tell me more."

"Leave the poor man alone, Karen. He didn't come here to be grilled about his personal life."

"It's okay," Nico said. And all of a sudden it was. He needed to say this stuff out loud. Maybe talking about it would help him make some kind of sense of it.

So he told them about Skye, about his discontent with retirement, about everything.

Here in this warm, welcoming place, he was beginning to see what was missing from his life. He needed anchors.

Home. Family. Work. Real, meaningful relationships. The stuff that made life worth living.

Somehow he'd managed to go racing through life so fast, he'd forgotten to stop and let any of the real living happen. And it was time to change that.

SKYE ADJUSTED the headset she wore and stared at the microphone inches from her mouth. If she looked at the radio DJ about to interview her, she was pretty sure she'd puke.

Four months had passed since she had boarded the bus to L.A. Four crazy, life-altering months. Not even in her wildest fantasies had she dared to believe that, at least in her professional life, her dreams would come true in spades.

The producer gave the sign that they were going live, and Skye cleared her mind of all puke-related thoughts.

"Today on *L.A. in Focus* we're talking to young-adult author Skye Ellison, whose first book hasn't even hit the shelves yet, and it already has major buzz and rumors of a movie in the making. Skye, welcome."

"Thanks, Jay. I'm glad to be here."

And terrified as hell.

But she reminded herself to breathe. No one had ever died from going on the radio…had they? Regardless, this probably wasn't going to kill her. She rehearsed in her head the points her publisher's PR person had reminded her to touch upon. She could do this.

God knew, she'd done worse.

"Tell us a little about your book and when it's going to hit stores," the DJ said.

"*The Cinderella Factor,* which will be released next March, is the first book in a series of teen novels about Emmy Walden, a sixteen-year-old from the valley who discovers she has the ability to time-travel while reading an old book of fairy tales to her baby sister. In this story, she gets stuck in a weird version of the story *Cinderella,* has to solve a mystery while she's there, and then figure out how to get back home in time for the homecoming dance."

"Sounds great, but writers everywhere are wondering how you've already gotten so much interest in the series before the first book has even hit the shelves."

"It was partly luck, partly being in the right place at the right time. Kid TV was looking for a show to target the preteen and early teen audience, and a friend introduced me to the CEO of the network. I pitched my book idea, and he loved it. The network hired people right away to start writing the scripts. It's been kind of a whirlwind few months, to say the least."

"What will the show be called, and when will the first episode air?"

"The show's name is *The Cinderella Factor*, same as my book, the first episode is scheduled for next month, July second at 2:00 p.m. Pacific Time, and it will be re-aired at 8:00 p.m. and midnight."

"So that explains your TV deal, but a movie, too? This must be unprecedented."

Skye got butterflies all over again, just thinking of how lucky she'd been. And of how much of it she owed to Nico.

"My agent managed to sell the movie rights to Blue Star Entertainment, and they want to capitalize on timing the movie close to the first book's release in the hope of creating cross-promotional buzz, so they've already gone into production and are shooting for a movie release of next summer."

"Wow, I don't think I've ever heard of simultaneous book-TV-movie deals happening to a brand-new author. How do you keep from letting it all intimidate you?"

"I just have to stay focused on the writing. I've got deadlines for the second and third books in the Emmy Walden series, and those help keep me thinking about what's important."

"I'll bet. For a writer, what's important is the writing, isn't it?"

"Absolutely. I don't let a day pass without sitting down and writing something."

"A lot of our listeners are aspiring authors and screenwriters themselves. What advice do you have to offer them?"

"Don't give up. If you keep writing, keep improving and keep submitting, someday you'll realize your dream. It's as simple as that."

"And it doesn't hurt if you've got friends introducing you to the heads of TV networks, right?"

Skye laughed. "Yes, I'm very thankful for my luck in that regard."

"I'd like to open up the lines to callers now. Listeners, if you have questions for Skye Ellison, author of the upcoming teen novel and media sensation, *The Cinderella Factor,* just dial 1-800…"

NICO'S STOMACH churned as he raced through a yellow light, praying his memory of the radio station's location was correct. Twelve blocks down, two more left turns, then a right, and he'd be there. He'd had to go there for a radio interview a few years back. She couldn't have been prerecorded, could she? If Skye was there taking calls right now?

At the end of the next block, he hit a red light, so he flipped open his cell phone and dialed the number the interviewer had given for calling in to Skye.

He had no idea what he'd say if he got on the air.

She probably wouldn't want to hear from him. Probably would hate him for interrupting her show like this. But he had to try.

One more time.

He knew now that he couldn't have his own happy ending without Skye in it. The truth had been simmering inside him for weeks—maybe even since he'd met her—but he'd needed this time alone to figure out who he was now and where he was going next.

Now that he knew that, he needed Skye. Hearing her voice on the radio talking about her book had cemented it. It had made him face a fact he'd been a little scared to face. Knowing he needed her was scary as hell when it was clear she didn't need him.

He got a busy signal, the light turned green, and he hit Redial as he followed the heavy traffic to the next stop. Now the line was ringing, only slightly louder than the pounding of his heart in his chest.

"How may I help you?" a female producer was asking him. "Hello? Are you calling to speak with our on-air author?"

Nico forced himself to speak. "Yes, I have a question for her."

"What's your name, location and question?"

"My name is Nico Valletti, I'm in L.A., and I'd like to ask her if she believes in happy endings," he blurted out of nowhere.

"Okay, I'll put you next in cue. Hold on a moment, please."

Nico waited on hold as the radio show played over the phone system. Skye was talking to another caller about the popularity of books for teens. And then he heard her thank the caller, a click on the line and his name being announced to the audience."

"Hello, Nico," the interviewer said. "What would you like to ask our author?"

SKYE'S MOUTH went dry, and she'd forgotten to breathe again. As she felt herself growing lightheaded and breathless, she inhaled deeply, then let it out slowly to avoid sounding like a heavy breather in her microphone.

Nico?

Why on earth would he call her here? And why now?

"Do you believe in happy endings?" she heard him ask.

"Yes, of course I do," she said, her voice sounding shaky to her own ears.

"If you were writing a story about us, don't you think we'd deserve one?"

She blinked away tears. If she were writing a story about herself and Nico, no one would believe it. The truth was too strange for fiction.

"I—"

"I'm sorry," the interviewer said, pressing a button on his console. "It appears we had a jokester calling. That'll be all our questions for now. When we return from our commercial break—"

Skye didn't hear what he said next. Her mouth hung open. The idiot had just hung up on the most romantic phone call she'd ever received. Why the hell did things like this always happen to her?

Her entire life was like a freaking warped fairy tale. Distorted, upside-down, inside-out—written by a medieval author on crack.

She stumbled her way through the rest of the interview on autopilot, plugging her book, answering questions, and an eternity later—well, probably more like ten minutes—she was finished.

Thoughts of Nico swirled around in her head. She'd tried hard not to think of him recently, and mostly, she'd succeeded. She'd been so busy, it was easy to get lost in writing and the business of writing. She'd let it all consume her, and it felt good not to think of what she couldn't have.

Ever since returning from the trip to Vegas, she'd been writing like a mad woman. Settling the score with Martin had cured her case of writer's block in a big way. And her writing had kept her from obsessing about what might have been with Nico.

But what could he want now? A happy ending? With her?

It sounded crazy. It sounded too good to be true. It sounded like the opposite of anything that might ever happen to Skye.

But hadn't that become the predominant theme in her life lately? Hadn't the unbelievable become commonplace? Hadn't she herself almost gotten used to saying things such as "I got a look at the script" and "my book's release date is being moved up because of the TV show?"

A few months ago, it would have sounded beyond impossible.

But somehow, some way, Skye had stepped into her own fantasies, and they were just as good as she'd imagined.

She left the offices of the radio station and walked out into the parking lot with her heart beating hard and fast. The bright sun caused her to squint, and she dug around in her bag for her sunglasses as she walked to her car.

The sound of tires squealing caught her attention, and she looked up to see a very familiar white Ferrari 360 Modena skidding to a halt six feet away.

Nico.

She blinked back tears as he climbed out of the car.

"What are you doing here?" she asked stupidly.

He closed the distance between them, his gaze locked on her with his trademark smoldering intensity. "I came to find you."

"Why'd you call in like that? I mean—"

She'd somehow become the queen of stupid questions, so she was thankful when he interrupted her. "I never should have let you leave Las Vegas. I should have told you then that I love you."

He was less than a foot away, standing there in all his hard-bodied glory, reminding Skye yet again that sometimes fantasies did come true. Sometimes, they even walked around and drove Ferraris.

His words finally registered in her brain, and she felt all her will to do the opposite melt away. This time, her instincts were screaming to go for it. She'd never wanted anything more than she wanted to trust herself this time.

But what if she was wrong? She always was. How could this time be any different?

Skye hovered, confused and indecisive, baffled by Nico's sudden change of heart.

"Why now?" she said.

"I'm sorry. I was stupid. I just…"

"Didn't want to go chasing after someone who insisted she didn't want you?"

Skye watched his reaction. His expression turned hard, then softened to amused.

"That was part of it. But I wasn't ready to believe what was going on between us."

"Which was what?"

"That we were falling in love. Or at least I was."

His vulnerability caused all the air to whoosh out of her lungs. How could she have walked away? But then, how could she trust what she was feeling now?

"I was, too," she said. "Or at least I think I was."

"Is this about that faulty instinct problem you think you have?"

Her gaze dropped to the asphalt parking lot beneath their feet. Skye never thought she'd come to a point in her doing-the-opposite strategy where doing the opposite would mean making the most painful choice in her life—walking away from the man she wanted most.

She couldn't answer.

"It is, isn't it? You're not giving yourself enough credit, Skye. Just because every other guy you've ever dated was an untrustworthy scumbag doesn't mean I am, too."

"I know you're not. But what if my instincts are telling me we're perfect together, and we're really not?"

"*I'm* telling you we're perfect together."

He reached out and took her by the waist, then pulled her close. He cupped her face with one hand and kissed her long and deep.

Was there any way to describe the way they felt together that was more appropriate than *perfect?*

"Does that feel right to you?" he whispered against her lips.

"Yes."

"Take a chance on us," he said. "We're worth it."

Skye closed her eyes and melted against him. Nico was right. Even if they crashed and burned, the chance of having her one big love was worth the risk.

"I love you," she said.

"I love you, too."

"That's all I need to know." Maybe Skye had finally gotten in touch with her smart instincts. Maybe the "maybes" were what made life worth living.

She took his hands in hers, and in his eyes, she could see the chance for their own happily ever after—the kind fantasies were made of.

Epilogue

"AREN'T YOU Skye Ellison, the author?"

Skye nodded at the cute guy in the tux and took a sip from her champagne flute, playing it casual.

"Wow, it's an honor to meet you," her companion said, extending his hand.

He bore a vague resemblance to the actor who played Emmy's romantic interest in *The Cinderella Factor* TV series.

Nico's charity benefit had been a huge success, judging by the black-tied and sequined crowd talking and drinking all around them. His primary goal had been to raise awareness of his new children's foundation, and no doubt, Race for Hope was going to become a favorite cause of celebs all over Hollywood by tomorrow morning.

Skye had lost track of Nico a few minutes ago and had contented herself standing on the sidelines, watching and listening. It was one of her favorite things to do at parties. But now there was the cute guy standing next to her, and he'd actually recognized her, so she couldn't very well ignore him.

She shook his hand. "And your name is?"

"Wil DiMario. I'm an actor."

Wasn't just about everybody here?

Skye smiled and nodded. "You look a little like the guy from *The Cinderella Factor* TV series."

"That's my brother," he said, smiling. "That's how I first heard of you—when he got the part on the show. And then I just saw you on CNN the other day talking about what it's like having your book go from TV series to movie so quickly."

Skye would never get used to being a minor celebrity. It was the reason most people came to L.A., but it hadn't ever really been her aspiration. Sure, she'd wanted to be known as a novelist, but it wasn't as though most novelists ever became the kind of people others recognized in public.

"It's been crazy, that's for sure," Skye said, just as she spotted Fiona and John across the room.

She'd been hoping they'd actually show up, though lately it had been hard to get the couple to remember anything besides each other. Skye had seen Fiona in more than a few relationships, but never anything like this. She focused on John the same way she focused when she was working on her collages—with an intensity that blocked out everything else.

"If you'll excuse me," she said to the actor, and he nodded and smiled as she headed in the direction of her friends.

"Hey," Fiona said as they embraced and pecked each other on the cheek. "You didn't tell me this place was going to look like the red carpet on Oscar night."

Skye hugged John, then took a step back to check out his and Fiona's attire. She'd seen her roommate's sparkly red dress on the hanger, but it looked much better on her friend.

"Wow, you look hot," she said, just as someone caught her around the waist.

"So do you," she heard Nico say in her ear.

They'd been together for six months now. Six crazy months, which had been sometimes sublime, sometimes taxing, sometimes exciting. But always real.

She no longer had to doubt her instincts, because for once they'd been right. Nico was the guy for her. They'd had their share of arguments, minor disasters and assorted other dramas, and they'd worked through it. Every day they got a little stronger, and every day she fell a little more in love with him.

"Can I borrow you for a few minutes?" he said after he'd hugged and shaken hands with her friends.

"Absolutely," she said, and he took her hand and led her to the stage, where an acid jazz band was playing a seriously funky riff.

When the music died down, he took the microphone, and Skye got a funny feeling in her belly. Somehow, she'd been duped. What the heck was she doing on stage, anyway?

She gave Nico's hand a tug, but he just flashed a mysterious smile and turned his attention back to the crowd down below.

"I just have a little announcement to make, and then everyone can get back to partying." The crowd quieted, and he continued. "You see, this woman here beside me happens to be the woman I love. Her name is Skye Ellison, and she doesn't know it yet, but I want to ask her to marry me."

Skye felt all the breath whoosh out of her lungs.

"I figured if I proposed in front of an audience, she'd have to say yes."

People laughed, clapped and cat-called.

Skye blinked away tears. With any other guy, standing on a stage hearing the most important question of her life would have been wrong, wrong, wrong.

But this was Nico, for whom none of the normal rules applied. And this was their relationship, in which the extraordinary was commonplace.

She heard herself laughing as tears streamed down her face.

"Skye, you are the most amazing woman I've ever met, and I don't want to spend a minute of my life without you. Will you marry me?"

She choked back tears and nodded, feeling like an idiot for not being about to answer out loud.

"Is that a yes?" he said, looking a little worried now.

"Yes," she said, finally recovering enough to speak. "Yes, yes, yes."

Her took her in his arms and kissed her then, as the crowd cheered below.

Skye wouldn't have dared to write such an improbably perfect ending for one of her own books, but as life had taught her lately, sometimes the truth was stranger than fiction. And sometimes, people really did get the chance to live happily ever after.

If you enjoyed what you just read,
then we've got an offer you can't resist!

Take 2 bestselling
love stories FREE!
Plus get a FREE surprise gift!

Clip this page and mail it to Harlequin Reader Service®

IN U.S.A.
3010 Walden Ave.
P.O. Box 1867
Buffalo, N.Y. 14240-1867

IN CANADA
P.O. Box 609
Fort Erie, Ontario
L2A 5X3

YES! Please send me 2 free Harlequin® Blaze™ novels and my free surprise gift. After receiving them, if I don't wish to receive anymore, I can return the shipping statement marked cancel. If I don't cancel, I will receive 6 brand-new novels each month, before they're available in stores! In the U.S.A., bill me at the bargain price of $3.99 plus 25¢ shipping and handling per book and applicable sales tax, if any*. In Canada, bill me at the bargain price of $4.47 plus 25¢ shipping and handling per book and applicable taxes**. That's the complete price and a savings of at least 10% off the cover prices—what a great deal! I understand that accepting the 2 free books and gift places me under no obligation ever to buy any books. I can always return a shipment and cancel at any time. Even if I never buy another book from Harlequin, the 2 free books and gift are mine to keep forever.

151 HDN D7ZZ
351 HDN D72D

Name	(PLEASE PRINT)	
Address	Apt.#	
City	State/Prov.	Zip/Postal Code

Not valid to current Harlequin® Blaze™ subscribers.

Want to try two free books from another series?
Call 1-800-873-8635 or visit www.morefreebooks.com.

* Terms and prices subject to change without notice. Sales tax applicable in N.Y.
** Canadian residents will be charged applicable provincial taxes and GST.
All orders subject to approval. Offer limited to one per household.
® and ™ are registered trademarks owned and used by the trademark owner and/or its licensee.

BLZ05   ©2005 Harlequin Enterprises Limited.

HARLEQUIN®

Blaze™

COMING NEXT MONTH

#243 OBSESSION Tori Carrington
Dangerous Liaisons, Bk. 2
Anything can happen in the Quarter.... Hotel owner Josie Villefranche knows that better than most. Ever since a woman was murdered in her establishment, business has drastically declined. She's very tempted to allow sexy Drew Morrison to help her take her mind off her troubles—until she learns he wants much more than just a night in her bed....

#244 WHAT HAVE I DONE FOR ME LATELY? Isabel Sharpe
It's All About Attitude
Jenny Hartmann's sizzling bestseller *What Have I Done for Me Lately?* is causing an uproar across the country. And now Jenny's about to take her own advice—by having a sexual fling with Ryan Masterson. What Jenny isn't prepared for is that the former bad boy is good in bed—and even better at reading between the lines!

#245 SHARE THE DARKNESS Jill Monroe
FBI agent Ward Cassidy thinks Hannah Garret is a criminal. And Hannah suspects Ward is working for her ex-fiancé, the man who now wants her dead. But when Hannah and Ward get caught for hours in a hot, darkened elevator, the sensual pull of their bodies tells them all they *really* need to know....

#246 MIDNIGHT OIL Karen Kendall
After Hours, Bk. 1
It's the trendiest salon in Miami...and landlord Troy Barrington is determined to shut it down. As part owner and massage therapist, Peggy Underwood can't let him—and his ego—win. So she'll use all of the sensual, er, *spa* tools at her disposal to change his mind.

#247 AFTERNOON DELIGHT Mia Zachary
Rei Davis is a tough-minded judge who wishes someone could see her softer side. Chris London is a lighthearted matchmaker who wishes someone would take him seriously. When Rei walks into Lunch Meetings, the dating service Chris owns, and the computer determines that they're a perfect match, sparks fly! But will all their wishes come true?

#248 INTO TEMPTATION Jeanie London
The White Star, Bk. 4
It's the sexiest game of cat and mouse she's ever played. MI6 agent Lindy Gardner is determined to capture Joshua Benedict—and the stolen amulet in his possession. The man is leading her on a sensual chase across two continents that will only make his surrender oh, so satisfying.